The Year of Small Shadow

The
Year
of
Small
Shadow

❦

EVELYN SIBLEY LAMPMAN

Harcourt Brace Jovanovich, Inc.

New York

The Year of Small Shadow

One

Small Shadow sat on the rough boards of the wagon box, his legs drawn up against his chest, and wondered what he would have for supper. Something good, of course. Maybe something he had never eaten before. Tom Smith said the whites ate many different things than the Indians on the reservation and that probably Small Shadow would grow tired of their food and be glad enough when it was time to come home. It could be true. Tom Smith knew the whites better than anyone else, but Small Shadow was quite willing to take the chance. The year ahead was going to be a great adventure. There wasn't an Indian on the Grande Ronde who wouldn't have traded places with him.

A cold rain had been falling ever since they left home. It had soaked through the blanket in which he had carefully wrapped himself, and his cotton shirt and pants were clammy cold against his body. He had worn his father's old felt hat, and the water collecting in the brim poured down in two steady streams from dips above each ear. He was too excited to notice.

He was a month late in arriving. They should have come at the time his father was sent away, but it was impossible then. The snows continued late in the year of 1880, and only men on horseback or afoot could get through. Chief Sam was too old and stiff to travel the fifteen miles between the reservation and Evansdale except by wagon, and as Chief of the Rogue Rivers it was Sam's duty to deliver Small Shadow to Dan'l Foster.

At last Tom Smith, who everybody agreed was the wisest man on the reservation, had announced that a wagon could get through, and he had been right, as usual.

It had been a hard trip. March was early to be traveling Oregon's dirt roads. Time after time the wheels had sunk hub-deep in mudholes, and they had to get out and help the horses by pushing and lifting. They had left at daylight, Tom and Chief Sam on the single seat, with Small Shadow riding in the wagon box. Now it was growing dusk, and Evansdale and Dan'l Foster lay just ahead.

He let himself think of Dan'l Foster. How surprised he would be when they arrived! Dan'l Foster didn't know they were coming. He didn't know that for one year he was going to have a son to work for him, to split wood and make fires and carry out his orders. They said Dan'l Foster had no squaw, and so a son would be a great help. Small Shadow resolved to be the best, the most devoted son a man ever had.

It wasn't as though he were going to a stranger. Everyone on the reservation knew and liked Dan'l Foster. He had visited with them often. He always had big copper pennies in his pocket, and sometimes on those visits he passed them out to children who happened to be in the agency store. He always gave Whisky Jim a silver piece when he begged—not the five dollars with which Whisky Jim always began his request, but sometimes as much as fifty cents.

Tom Smith said that Whisky Jim and a few of the others who begged for money were bad. He said they gave all of the Indians a bad name. The whites remembered only the bad and forgot the good. He had talked to Small Shadow about this a long time before they left, and Small Shadow had promised never to beg for anything. There were other words of advice, too, but Small Shadow thought begging was the most important. He wouldn't want to shame Dan'l Foster in any way.

Dan'l Foster was a lawyer, and when the reservation people had trouble with the law, they always went to him. He never let them down. Lew Youngbuck, Small Shadow's father, had gone to him with that problem of the roan stallion. Because it was Dan'l Foster who talked for him in court, Lew would be gone only a year, not for five or ten as was customary when an Indian stole from a white man.

Dan'l had convinced the jury that Lew had not meant to keep the stallion. He had only borrowed it to breed with a mare, but had forgotten to ask permission first. Small Shadow did not think that this was so, but all the Indians who were present at the trial did. They had not thought of it before Dan'l Foster pointed it out, but now they were sure that was the way it happened.

The wagon swerved slightly, and he saw that they had reached the crossroads. Winding east was the muddy road to Salem, the state capital. They turned south, jolting and sloshing through the last stretch before reaching Evansdale.

Small Shadow shook his head, dislodging a small cloudburst from the hat brim, and sniffed with excitement. They were about to pass the tannery! Everyone on the reservation had laughed when Tom Smith told them the funny story he had heard about it. Cody Pugh, the owner, had been asked to build his tannery outside of town. Some of the white women objected to the stench of drying leather!

Small Shadow didn't object. He thought it smelled fine and sniffed with delight as they rolled past.

With a jolt, the rain-washed landscape on either side disappeared behind splintery boards. Above their heads was the protecting roof of the covered bridge that spanned Echo Creek. When they came out on the other side, they would be in Evansdale! Small Shadow could hardly sit still. It was all he could do to keep from jumping out and running ahead of the horses.

He had been here before. When he was younger, before his mother died, he had often accompanied her as she went from door to door selling the baskets she had made or the wild berries she had picked. Later, he had come twice with his father on the Fourth of July, when Indian horse races were part of the celebration. Each time he had studied Evansdale—the only town he had ever seen—carefully, but today he was seeing it through new eyes. For one year it was to be his home.

There was one main street, and all the interesting places were strung along on either side of three blocks. On his left was a livery barn, where some of the rich whites kept horses. Next to it was the blacksmith shop, and even in the cold rain the double doors were open. As they jolted by, Small Shadow had a glimpse of the smithy's fire, glowing red in the dark interior. He could not look as long as he would have liked. He had to turn his head quickly to see the opposite side of the street.

Here were three small buildings, the first occupied by a man who sawed and hammered wood, creating chairs and tables. Sometimes he even made houses. The second belonged to a man who made harnesses and saddles, and the third was a strange place that Tom Smith called a newspaper. Once a week in this building a huge machine made black marks on large white papers, and Tom Smith said that the sound was frightening at first, but you soon got used to it. Small

Shadow could hardly wait for the day the machine was put to work. He wouldn't be scared, not since Tom Smith had assured him it was harmless.

Again he turned his head, for the wagon had rolled through a rutty intersection. He allowed himself a brief glimpse of the courthouse square. The courthouse sat in the very middle of the block, with one huge, bare-limbed oak in the surrounding yard. Small Shadow tried not to look at it. It was called the Hanging Tree, and once, many years ago, a man had gone to his death from a rope looped over one of the limbs.

He turned back quickly, for the western side of this block was the most interesting in town. Here the places of business were built solidly together, with no space in between. There was a general store, much like the one on the reservation, but with a larger, finer stock and one that never ran out; a curious place in which a white man scraped the beards from other whites who were too lazy to do it for themselves; and a second carpenter's shop. Sandwiched between that and the largest establishment on the far corner, a place called a saloon, which sold whisky and so was forbidden to the Indians, was Dan'l Foster's office. They were here at last!

Tom Smith grunted to the team, and as it came to a halt, the two old nags drooped their heads with exhaustion. There was no need to fasten them to the hitching rail, which extended the full length of the block. They were too tired to go farther.

Struggling with the folds of the sodden blanket, Small Shadow got to his feet and jumped down in the road. He was not surprised that one of his feet had gone to sleep, and he stomped up and down, the mud oozing through his bare toes. It reminded him that he mustn't forget his shoes, and he reached back in the wagon box. They had grown too small, and he could no longer get them on his feet, but he had brought them anyway. It did not seem right to come to Dan'l Foster without any shoes.

As he stood waiting for the men to climb down from the seat, he looked across the intersection toward the third block. To him, this was the least interesting, for it contained mainly churches. There were two of them, one on each side of the street, with small houses at the sides that Tom Smith said were occupied by the ministers.

Facing him, on the side street opposite the courthouse, was the jail. It was a two-storied frame building with bars at the upper windows. Small Shadow knew about the jail. After the Independence Day horse races, many Indians spent the night behind its doors.

By now Tom Smith and Chief Sam were both on the ground. Like Small Shadow, they were soaked through. Rain streamed from their hat brims, and their blankets clung to their bent shoulders. They were both old men, and the years had taken toll of their strength. When they were tired, as now, they no longer stood straight and tall.

They plodded through the mud and stepped up onto the boardwalk that ran before the block of business houses. There was a moment's hesitation, and Small Shadow knew it was the delicate matter of who should lead. Sam was Chief of the Rogue Rivers on the reservation, and Small Shadow was of his tribe. Tom Smith was not a Rogue River. He was a Chinook, and not even a chief. But Tom Smith knew the whites, and some of them even called him friend. To undertake this mission without him would have been impossible.

Tom decided the matter by falling back. Chief Sam should have the honored position in the lead. Tom was content to be second, and Small Shadow would bring up the rear. In that manner they progressed single file to the entrance of Dan'l Foster's office, where Tom reached forward and boldly opened the door.

No one had lighted a lamp, and at first Small Shadow found it impossible to see inside the gloomy interior. It was like entering a black cave. But it was warm. Heat rushed out to meet them, and when Tom Smith gently pushed Chief Sam forward, Small Shadow was glad to follow. His nose wrinkled momentarily at the offensive odor of the white man that filled the room. That would be the hardest thing to endure in the year ahead.

At first their arrival was greeted by silence; then the familiar voice of Dan'l Foster came from the darkness.

"Chief Sam! Tom! Come in. I say, come in and set a spell. Whatever brings you out in weather fit only for a duck?"

There was commotion in the darkness, the stir of someone bustling around, the scratch of a sulfur match, the tiny flare that grew into a larger, spreading light as Dan'l Foster lit a coal-oil lamp. Then the lawyer was stepping forward with extended hand to greet his visitors.

He was not a big man, but he had broad shoulders and large hands and feet. His graying hair fell just below his ears and looked as though it had been trimmed to conform with the edges of a bowl turned upside down upon his head. He had a large nose, an angular face, and shrewd blue eyes beneath overhanging brows.

Chief Sam and Tom Smith let their wet blankets drop to the floor and solemnly shook hands. They ignored Small Shadow, but Dan'l Foster's sharp eyes found him, leaning against the door.

"Come in, son," he said kindly. "Drop your blanket and find yourself a place next to the stove. You'll never dry out way back there."

Despite his chattering teeth, Small Shadow felt warmed by Dan'l Foster's words. He had called him son! It was almost as though he had guessed. He gathered up the blankets dropped by Tom Smith and Chief Sam, spreading them out so they might dry a little. As he did so, he cast a quick glance at Dan'l Foster, hoping that the white man would notice. In small services like this could a son be useful to a man when there were no squaws around to do the work.

But Dan'l Foster did not notice. He was busy introducing the older Indians to a white man who occupied a chair close to the round stove.

"This is Rufus Gadsby, one of Evansdale's leading citizens," he was saying. "Rufe, you know Tom Smith from the reservation. And this is Chief Sam. Sam's chief of the fifty-eight Rogue Rivers that stayed on at the Grande Ronde when the rest of the tribe was moved to the Siletz."

Rufus Gadsby was short and plump, with a fringe of white hair encircling his bald head. In the lamplight his skin looked very pink, and his round eyes shone with curiosity. He stepped forward eagerly to extend his hand.

Both of the older Indians gravely shook hands before selecting one of the straight-backed chairs that circled the stove. After this the four sat for some moments in courteous silence, enjoying the fire.

Small Shadow was reluctant to accept Dan'l Foster's invitation to join the circle. He knew that Tom

Smith could call him forward at the proper time, but the subject must not be rushed into headlong. That would be impolite. He stayed where he was, at the outer fringe of heat cast by the stove, his eyes busily darting from side to side.

Dan'l Foster's law office was not large and was only a single room. The round stove, its sides glowing red, occupied the center. The circle of unpainted chairs, with seats of laced rawhide, took up most of the floor space. There was only room for a desk, littered with a mound of papers, against one wall, and a small bookcase against another.

On the floor, at intervals spaced for the convenience of occupants of the chairs, were three spittoons, filled to the brim with black liquid that Small Shadow knew was tobacco juice. They looked ready to overflow, but as he watched, the man called Rufus Gadsby turned his head and aimed a stream at the closest spittoon. It hit the mark and the surface quivered, but none slopped over the edge.

"A bad day," said Dan'l Foster finally.

"Cold. Much rain," agreed Tom Smith.

"But better than that snow that hung on so long," added Rufus Gadsby. "Never seen snow hang on so long as it did this year."

"Much snow." Tom Smith nodded agreeably. The slight motion dislodged a pool of rainwater that had collected in his hat brim, and it ran down his shoulders.

"You ought to take off your hats and give them a good shaking," advised Mr. Gadsby solicitously.

Dan'l Foster frowned, and Small Shadow caught his breath. Tom Smith never removed his hat in public. When he was a baby, his mother had fastened a board over his forehead to the crown of his head, and the soft bones had grown to a malformed point. It had been a custom of the old Chinooks and was considered a mark of beauty. Now it was no longer done, and Tom Smith was ashamed. He did not like people to know about his head.

"Forgive my friend," said Dan'l Foster in the trade jargon known to all the far-western tribes. "In some things he is a man without sense, but his heart is good."

Rufus Gadsby's pink, round face grew puzzled. It was clear that he did not realize he had made a social blunder and equally clear that he did not understand jargon. He looked from one to another of the faces about the stove, two brown and creased with wrinkles, gray braids hanging below their dripping hats, the third lighter skinned and with watchful blue eyes below bristling bows.

"It's the only sensible thing to do," he insisted. "Why shouldn't they take off their hats, Dan'l? And give them a good shake to get rid of the rain? Anybody'd—"

"Hush up, Rufe," ordered Dan'l Foster gently, but there was a certain quality in his tone that caused the words to die in the other's mouth. "You can set if you've a mind to, or you can leave. But if you stay, you keep your mouth clamped up."

"I'll set a while longer," declared Rufe Gadsby instantly.

"It is a long ride from the reservation. The roads are deep mud." Again Dan'l Foster spoke in jargon as he turned back to the Indians. "Your errand is important. I hope there is no great trouble."

"There is no trouble," Chief Sam confirmed in the same tongue. For the first time since they entered, he seemed at ease.

It had been a shock to all of them to find that Dan'l Foster had a visitor. Of course, what would transpire would soon be public knowledge, but the initial proceedings were for Dan'l's ears alone. If the other white stayed on and Dan'l included him in the conversation, the whole matter would have to be explained by Tom Smith. Chief Sam understood English well enough, but like many of the older Indians on the reservation, he pretended that he didn't. It was easier that way. When a white man asked him a question, it need not be answered.

Now Dan'l had settled things by speaking jargon. He had also told the white man that he was free to leave.

"Still the matter is of some importance." Dan'l probed gently. "Otherwise, Chief Sam and Tom Smith would not be here in this weather."

"It is important. We bring you your son. Your son for the year," announced Chief Sam.

Dan'l Foster, who was usually so filled with words, found none. His mouth dropped open without sound.

Tom Smith motioned Small Shadow forward.

"Lew Youngbuck, for whom you spoke before the judge, gives you his son for the year he is to be away. Lew Youngbuck is a good man. Honest. He has no money to pay you for your talk. His son will pay with the work he does for you."

"I see." Dan'l Foster's shrewd eyes grew even more knowing. The smile that he turned on Small Shadow was one of kindness. "There is no need. Your father is a good man, son, and I appreciate him trying to pay his bill this way. But there is no bill. Gabe Buell got his horse back, and your father got off with only a year to serve. No harm was done. You do not have to work for me. You go back to the reservation with Chief Sam and Tom. The year will be up before you know it, and your father will be home."

"No!" objected Chief Sam and Tom Smith in a single voice. Tom fell silent, allowing the chief to speak.

"Lew Youngbuck sent me word," explained Sam. "From the penitentiary in the place called Salem. The word was brought by Jim Sharp, who just returned from there. Jim Sharp says it is a fine place, this penitentiary. He had to work, but it was not squaw's work. He made bricks, and other men did the same. Three times a day he was given food. At night he slept on a bed with a blanket in a room with no rain coming through the roof. He met many people. Made many friends. They gave him new clothes. Shoes, too. Bad men were punished with heavy balls chained to their legs, but Jim was not bad. It did not happen to him. He saw much that was strange and has many stories to tell of his experiences."

"Most people don't think so highly of the penitentiary," said Dan'l Foster dryly. "They don't like it at all. But Jim was a model prisoner. That made things easier."

"Lew Youngbuck sent word that while he is gone, his son will be your son," insisted Chief Sam. "He will learn many things, too."

"He will be paying Lew's debt," put in Tom Smith. "Lew has no money. No one has money on the reservation. Dan'l Foster does not ask for money, but it is right that we should pay. It is honest and fair."

"Are you trying to tell me that from now on every time I defend somebody on the reservation, I'm going to have to support his young'uns if I don't get him off?" Dan'l Foster turned to Tom, and this time he spoke in English, running the words together fast in the hope that Chief Sam couldn't follow. "Is that why you're trying to give me this boy?"

"No," denied Tom quickly. "But Small Shadow has no one else. There's only him and Lew living on that land way out at the edge of the reservation. Look at him, Dan'l Foster. He is small. He has no one."

"Someone on the reservation could take him in." Dan'l frowned. "He's a Rogue River, and Chief Sam has plenty of families who could make room."

"No room," declared Sam loudly in jargon. "Lew Youngbuck send his son to Dan'l Foster. If you do not take him, he will starve. I will give orders. No Rogue River will take Small Shadow."

"There are other Indians. Other tribes besides the Rogue Rivers at Grande Ronde," Dan'l reminded him. "Lots of Chinooks, Kalapooias, Yamhills, Molalas—"

"They will not take him," insisted Chief Sam. "Not when I spread the word."

Rufus Gadsby could stand it no longer. He had caught enough of the brief interlude in English to grasp what was going on.

"You mean to say, Dan'l, they're trying to give you this Injun boy? Don't they know that slavery's unlawful since the war?"

"They're not giving him to me for a slave, Rufe. And not forever. They want me to keep him for a year while his pa's in the pen," explained Dan'l, frowning at the interruption.

Small Shadow's heart thumped so hard that it was like a drum in his ears. He couldn't believe it. Dan'l Foster didn't want him! He was refusing the offer of a son who had meant to do so much for him. He wanted Small Shadow to go home, back to the reservation to face the jeers of those who had congratulated him on his good fortune. He stepped forward, his muddy feet leaving wet tracks on the board floor.

"Do not send me back," he begged. The words of advice given by Tom Smith returned to him. "I will work for you. I will never beg for anything. When the whites turn their heads away, I will not mind. I will feel no anger. I will smile and try to do good to them. I will wash myself clean and try to bring honor on you. I will sleep in the hay with your horse and eat only what is left after you have finished. But do not send me back, Dan'l Foster. The others will laugh because you did not want me. I cannot go back to be laughed at."

"What's your name, son?" Dan'l Foster looked at him carefully.

"His name is *Tenas Polakely*, Small Shadow." Chief Sam answered for him. "Lew Youngbuck has given him no other."

"But if Dan'l Foster wants to give him a new name, he can," put in Tom Smith hastily.

"You know you can't keep him, Dan'l," Rufe reminded him quickly. "What'll folks say? An Injun boy running around Evansdale as free as the air! It's unheard of. You'd best send him packing. The men'll be bad enough, but when the womenfolk get wind of it, they'll skin you alive. Maybe run you and him both out of town."

Dan'l Foster had never taken his eyes from Small Shadow's face. It was as though no one else had spoken. Now he smiled, a smile that started in his eyes, spread to the little wrinkles at the corners and down into his cheeks and mouth. The wild drumming of Small Shadow's heart began to die away.

"He can stay," he told Chief Sam and Tom. And to Rufus Gadsby, "I say, he's going to stay. I've made up my mind. We'll cross each bridge when we come to it and not before."

Two

〄

"This here's where I live," explained Dan'l Foster, coming to a halt on the single plank that served as a walkway. "It don't belong to me. It belongs to Old Lady Hicks. I say, it's her house, and she keeps boarders."

Small Shadow's eyes tried to penetrate the darkness, but without moon or stars it was difficult to see. He could make out the square bulk of a frame building, but nothing more. No lights were visible in the front.

It had been a busy hour since his arrival in Evansdale. Once Dan'l Foster had made his decision, he had concerned himself with the comfort of the older Indians. He had waved aside Tom Smith's polite assertion that they meant to spend the night in the wagon. Dan'l would hear of no such thing. The team had been taken to the livery stable, and he had dug into his own pocket for coins to pay for oats. Tom Smith had protested politely, but not too much, and Small Shadow realized that Tom had not begged.

Then they had retraced their steps, pausing before the general store. The Indians waited in the rain while Dan'l went inside. When he returned, he carried a paper bag, which he handed to Chief Sam. The chief had not opened it, but Small Shadow knew that it contained food for their supper. Again, it had been a freewill offering. No one had begged for food.

Last of all, Dan'l had led the way to the courthouse, where he had spoken with certain white men. The Indians stood back, and Small Shadow had been unable to overhear their words, but in the end, one of the men called Sheriff Tombs had led them across the street to the jail. Chief Sam and Tom Smith would spend the night there under cover, but it was not as though they had done something wrong. It was only shelter until daylight when they would be free to leave for the reservation.

When all this was completed, they had shaken hands all around, and Dan'l had conducted Small Shadow to his new home. It was not far, just across a side street and catty-corner from the back of the courthouse. The house sat by itself on the block, but he could see faint lights on the north and south, which meant there were other dwellings beyond.

"Now before we go in, there's one or two things I should tell you." Dan'l spoke slowly, choosing his words with care. "White ladies is different from Indians. I say, they're as different as day and night. Some of them you can't tell to do a thing and expect them to do it. They got to be managed around. Most times, it's got to be their idea or they'll rear back and balk like a mule. Now you take Old Lady Hicks. She's got a good heart, soft as butter in July, but she don't like folks to know about it. And she's got a tongue that stings like a wasp, but you mustn't give it no mind."

Small Shadow nodded. The squaw who kept house for Dan'l Foster would be difficult. Tom Smith had already prepared him for such things.

"Now you let me do the talking," ordered Dan'l sternly. "I say, you keep a quiet tongue in your head. And don't take everything I might say to heart, neither. Chances are I don't mean a word of it. Just trust me, son. I say, trust me and things'll work out all right."

He turned and led the way around the side of the house toward the rear, and Small Shadow trotted after, his bare feet sinking in the thick mud.

Light was coming through the back windows. It spread itself far enough so he could see that there were other buildings on the lot besides a residence. The closest was for storing wood, for through the open door he could make out a chopping block, with an ax handle sticking out at an angle. Beyond that was a privy, and still beyond a larger bulk that he judged to be a barn.

The back door was approached by a wide porch, and here Dan'l halted again and began manipulating the handle of a pump, which eventually produced a stream of water. He filled a shallow basin, set upon a ledge, and motioned Small Shadow toward a dish filled with soft soap.

"We have to wash up before we go in," he explained. "Mrs. Hicks—and don't forget and call her Old Lady to her face—would just send us back if we forgot."

Small Shadow dipped his fingers in the soap and then in the water. It was icy cold, but he tried to do as good a job as he could at cleansing his face and hands. Last of all, he washed his muddy feet.

Tom Smith claimed that cleanliness was important to some of the whites. Small Shadow was glad. Like most Rogue Rivers he liked to be clean. Before they were taken from their former home and brought to the reservation, they had bathed daily in the river. Now it was more difficult. The river here was small. In summer it was shallow and filled with slimy mud.

"Mrs. Hicks sets great store by this pump," explained Dan'l chattily as he awaited his turn. "I say, there's not more'n a half dozen in town. Most folks still draw well water with a bucket. Wouldn't hurt a mite to tell her you admire it."

Small Shadow stored away the information. He had seen pumps before, but only from a distance. On the reservation there were some wells, but as often as not water was still carried from the river. He dried himself on the soggy roller towel and stood back waiting respectfully.

Dan'l did not waste much time at his ablutions. He dipped into the water gingerly, pawed at the damp towel, wiped his feet on the rag rug at the threshold, then boldly threw open the kitchen door. Small Shadow trailed close behind.

Two women occupied the room, and neither of them turned at the opening of the door. The younger was stirring something on the stove, while the other bent to peer inside the dark oven.

Dan'l struggled out of his coat and motioned that Small Shadow would remove his dripping blanket. He hung them and their hats on pegs driven into the wall beside the cupboard.

"Did you wipe your feet good, Dan'l? I'll not have mud tracked onto my clean floor." The voice was muffled as its owner began sliding something from the oven. Small Shadow sniffed with delight at the new smell, so sweet and spicy.

"Yes'm, Mrs. Hicks," said Dan'l meekly. "Wiped my feet on the mat and washed at the pump. I say, we both of us did."

"Both?" Mrs. Hicks carefully set a deep plate covered with brown crust on the table, then whirled around.

Small Shadow observed that she was a tall woman, very thin, and one who gave the impression of a rainy day. Her long cotton dress was gray, so was the straight hair, pulled back and up to a knot atop her head, so were the eyes, at first wide with surprise, but slowly narrowing with a new emotion. Even her skin was sallow and without color.

"Who's that?" she demanded shrilly. "Dan'l Foster, have you taken leave of your senses? What do you mean bringing a Injun into my house?"

"Only a little one, Mrs. Hicks. You can see for yourself, he's no bigger'n a half pint. He's got no place else to go. And since, in a way, it's my doing, I figured it was my Christian duty to bring him home."

"You're a fine one to be talking about Christian duty, Dan'l Foster!" This was a new voice, and Small Shadow saw that the doorway leading to the next room was now filled by a strange man. "You, who never sets foot in church saving on Christmas or Easter, and not even then lessen Mrs. Hicks makes you go. What do you know about Christian duty?"

"You stay out of this, Jacob Riley," ordered Mrs. Hicks without turning her head. "Go back and set some more. We'll call you for supper when it's ready. What do you mean it's your duty, Dan'l?"

"I sent the boy's pa up to the pen," explained Dan'l sadly. "You remember Lew Youngbuck? The one that had trouble with Gabe Buell about a horse?"

"Course I remember. He stole that horse, Dan'l, and you know it," she reminded him tartly. "Even the jury knowed it. You just hoodwinked 'em into giving that Injun a short sentence, not what he deserved at all. And if he's this young'un's pa, that makes things even worse. You figure I'd want the son of a jailbird in my kitchen?"

"No, ma'am," said Dan'l humbly. "Maybe he could stay in the barn. You never use it anyway. He could bed down in that old, moldy hay. It's good enough for the likes of him, I reckon. And whatever's left over from supper, I'll carry out for him to eat. It's not as though you had a pig to eat up the slops."

"Whatever are you saying?" she demanded crossly, taking long strides across the kitchen to inspect the boy more closely. "Look at him. Thin as a rail. Probably hasn't had a good meal in his whole life. A cold barn would bring on a fever afore you could bat your eye. It'd be the death of him."

"What the Lord giveth He taketh away," remarked Jacob Riley mournfully.

"He's got to stay somewhere," Dan'l told her helplessly. "They won't take him back on the reservation —not till his pa gets home. And since I sent him there, they brought the boy to me. I don't know what to do, Mrs. Hicks. I say, it'll take a wiser head than mine to figure it out."

"What's his name?" she demanded, frowning. "Or does he have a real name, not one of them outlandish things they sometimes call theirselves?"

"Name's Sm— His name is Shad," amended Dan'l quickly.

"Shad? You mean like the fish? Or is it short for something?"

Dan'l hesitated, but Jacob Riley spoke up triumphantly.

"There, you see, Dan'l! That just goes to prove

you're no good Christian. Anybody that reads his Bible knows that Shad is short for Shadrach. Shadrach, Meshach, and Abednego. Them's the three that went down into the fiery furnace. At least it goes to show that the boy's folks had some Bible learning. What church do you lean to, boy?"

"You must be right, Jacob!" There was admiration and some relief in Dan'l's tone. "Shad's bound to be short for Shadrach, though I never thought of it. Mrs. Hicks, what do you figure I should do?"

"I'm thinking on it," she told him grimly. "And until I decide, we best eat supper. I'm glad to see that Bertha's gone right ahead dishing up, so we'll go in to the table."

"Shad, too?" asked Dan'l slyly. "Or maybe he'd better carry a plate outside in the rain."

"Of course, Shad too." She frowned. "And I'll hear no more nonsense about him eating slops."

It was the most delicious meal Small Shadow could remember. Dan'l was careful to announce each dish by name before he passed it on, and Small Shadow carefully filed the information away in his mind. He would never tire of this food, he decided.

Tom Smith had warned him that white squaws were particular and did not approve of using only a knife and fingers at their meals, so Small Shadow watched Mrs. Hicks carefully. He used the same utensils she did, fingers for the spareribs, bread, and pickles, a spoon for the gravy and the peas, the more

32

difficult fork for the string beans and the apple pie. He said nothing while he ate, and when the bowls and platters went around the second and third times, he always looked at Mrs. Hicks, waiting to be urged before helping himself to another serving.

"He's got table manners at least," declared his hostess. "I don't know who learned him to eat, but I couldn't have done a better job myself."

They arose from the table, and while Bertha, the hired girl, began clearing the table, Mrs. Hicks led the way to the sitting room. Dan'l winked reassuringly at Small Shadow behind her back. His smile said that things were going well.

Even before they sat down, Bertha opened the back door for a visitor. It was a lady whom the others called Dulcy. She was the wife of Rufus Gadsby, the man Small Shadow had met in Dan'l's office. Like her husband, she was small and plump, with white hair. As soon as she entered the room, she began talking.

"I hope I'm not in the way, Mrs. Hicks, but I did want to return this crochet pattern before I lost it. You know how I am—always hiding things away to keep them safe. Then I forget where I hid them. Evening, Dan'l. Evening, Jacob. Rain's stopped, you'll be glad to hear."

"But it's still mighty wet and dark out, Dulcy," Mrs. Hicks reminded her. "You could have waited till morning with the pattern, like you generally do. You couldn't have lost it in that time."

"So that's the boy." Dulcy Gadsby ignored the remark. Her eyes fastened themselves on Small Shadow. "Rufe told me all about him. My, but it's sad, and him so young and all."

"What's sad?" demanded Mrs. Hicks suspiciously.

"Why, about them trying to give him to Dan'l as a slave. As if slaves was allowed in this country any more."

"Rufe's got it wrong as usual." Mrs. Hicks's voice was smug. "Shad's no slave. He's just a little boy, a little Injun boy with no family, excepting a pa that's locked up for a year. They just want Dan'l to look after him till his pa gets out. That's all."

"Now that's what I call real gall," declared Dulcy Gadsby indignantly. "As if Dan'l was responsible! That's what we got the reservation for, to look after the Injuns. 'Twouldn't be decent for the boy to stay here in town. Everybody knows that."

"What's indecent about it, I'd like to know?" demanded Mrs. Hicks wrathfully. "It ain't all settled, but if Dan'l wants to pay his board and if I decide to take Shad in as a boarder, I can't see who is likely to stop me. Maybe he's got a red skin, not a freckled one like yours, Dulcy Gadsby, but you'd look a long way before you'd find somebody with better manners at the table."

"We are all brothers under the skin," Jacob Riley reminded them.

Before Mrs. Gadsby could recover from her surprise, Bertha ushered in another visitor. This was Mrs. Clifford, wife of the county judge, who had been one of the men with whom Dan'l had conferred in the courthouse. Mrs. Clifford had come to borrow a cup of sugar.

"I didn't realize I was out until after Onnie Hatcher closed up his store," she told them. As she spoke, her eyes studied Small Shadow, sitting stiffly in his chair beside Dan'l.

"You got plenty of sugar, Almira Clifford. You just wanted to see the boy," accused Mrs. Gadsby. "And now you seen him. You'll have plenty more chances, too, because Mrs. Hicks has just about made up her mind to let him stay here. You know how it is when Mrs. Hicks makes up her mind. Nobody can change her."

"I can," declared Mrs. Clifford angrily. "As the wife of the duly elected judge of this county, I've got certain rights. I won't have an Indian boy living in our town, trying to play with our children. I'm going right home and tell the judge that he's got to do something about it."

"There's nothing he can do, Mrs. Clifford," Dan'l told her quickly. "Not if Mrs. Hicks lets him stay and if I make myself responsible. I say, there's nothing in the law that says Shad can't live here."

Small Shadow was having trouble keeping up with changing events. He was not worried because Dan'l Foster had said to trust him. Still the others were very confusing. They kept changing sides. First Mrs. Hicks said he had to go; now she claimed that he might stay. Mrs. Gadsby, too, had seemed against it at first, but the gloating smile with which she now watched Mrs. Clifford led him to believe that she also might be changing her mind. Jacob Riley had given no opinion one way or another, but no one seemed to pay much attention to him anyway. He kept his eyes on Mrs. Clifford's face, marveling how it seemed to grow redder by the minute.

"Look at him!" declared Mrs. Clifford scornfully. "Dirty! Unwashed! Ragged!"

"He washed before supper," contradicted Mrs. Hicks. "I seen some of my soft soap still sticking to the side of his face. As for his clothes, I mean to scrub them out tomorrow."

"The ladies of the Methodist Missionary Society might take on the job of making him some new clothes," said Mrs. Gadsby thoughtfully. "We do lots of sewing for the heathen afar. 'Twouldn't hurt one mite to sew for one closer to hand. They'll all want to get a look at him, anyway."

"Charity beginneth at home," Jacob Riley commented.

"The Methodists don't do a bit more for the heathen than the Baptists," declared Mrs. Clifford quickly. "Our Missionary Society's just filled a whole barrel for the heathen. There's probably a lot of things he could wear if he has to stay. And I could see to it because I happen to be president."

"The Methodists would sew *new* clothes," Mrs. Gadsby reminded her. "No hand-me-downs that's all but wore out."

"Can you sew new shoes? Look at his feet! Bare as the day he was born, and in this weather, too. There's bound to be a pair of shoes to fit him in the barrel. Of course, I still think he should go back to the reservation where he belongs," concluded Mrs. Clifford.

Dan'l stood up.

"We'll leave you ladies to work things out," he told them. "Shad here's had a hard day. I say, he was up early and he had a long ride. Maybe he'd like to turn in."

"Give him one of your shirts to sleep in, Dan'l," ordered Mrs. Hicks. "And put his own clothes in the hall, so Bertha can get them for the wash. Shad's to have the little room next to you. The bed's all made up."

Three

Small Shadow spent the following day confined to the kitchen while Mrs. Hicks and Bertha laundered his pants and shirt. Since they were the only clothing he owned, he wore one of Dan'l's shirts. It was a fine garment, without a single tear or patch, but it was much too large and came well below his knees. He didn't mind that, but it was hard to have to sit quietly in the steamy kitchen when he wanted to explore the town.

Just before noon, Dulcy Gadsby stopped by. From his chair in the corner, Small Shadow smiled at her shyly, but she was too overflowing with news to notice. She had spent the morning contacting the members of the Methodist missionary ladies, and they had agreed to sew the following day.

"Which is more than the Baptists will do," she concluded. "I bet you a cooky Almira Clifford's clean forgot she promised to dig in her barrel for shoes."

"I've not heard from her yet, but I'll call it to her mind," promised Mrs. Hicks. "You holding the sewing bee at your house, Dulcy?"

"Oh, no." Mrs. Gadsby seemed a little startled. "So long as the boy's already here and you don't mind it, we thought we'd bring our thimbles over to your house. Several of the ladies have got extra piece goods that they're willing to donate, and Mrs. Flint is bringing a pattern that she uses for her own boys that ought to work real good. And I've got—"

"Stop your clattering, Dulcy Gadsby!" Small Shadow was surprised that Mrs. Hicks looked suddenly angry. He thought it was very nice of Mrs. Gadsby to go to so much trouble for him. "What you're trying to say is that my house is already contaminated," she declared. "And you don't want yours to be. Don't try to cover up with all them donations and good intentions. I got the idea right off."

Small Shadow was puzzled about the word contaminated. He wondered what it meant.

"Of course if you'd rather not have the sewing bee—" began Mrs. Gadsby stiffly.

"Oh, we'll have it," Mrs. Hicks told her firmly. "We'll have it right here. You come with your thimbles and your piece goods after breakfast and sew through the day. And while you're about it, make sure some is suitable for underwear, for he's not got a stitch to his name."

"No underwear!" For the first time Mrs. Gadsby turned to stare at Small Shadow, and there was something in her eyes that made him uncomfortable. Lots of people had no underwear, he told himself. It was cooler without it in summer, and in winter there were always blankets, sometimes buckskin jackets.

"It'll be just like sewing for the heathen in darkest Africa. You'll have to provide from the skin out," Mrs. Hicks reminded her. "Although maybe the Baptist barrel has some underwear. I could ask Mrs. Clifford if you want."

"No," declared Mrs. Gadsby quickly. "We'll take care of everything. You leave it to us, Mrs. Hicks." She stood up, gathering her shawl about her shoulders. "I must run now. There's more to do for tomorrow than ever I thought."

At the door she paused and looked back at Small Shadow. She did not smile, nor did he. He stared back at her defiantly. He had decided that he didn't like Mrs. Gadsby.

It took most of the day for his heavy cotton pants to dry. Mrs. Hicks had spread them over the back of a chair next to the wood stove, and from time to time she kept turning them. By late afternoon she pronounced them ready to iron, and Bertha put a heavy flatiron on the stove to heat.

Small Shadow had never seen anyone iron clothes, and he found it very interesting.

"But why do you do it?" he asked. "They will wrinkle again when I wear them."

"I iron when the missus tells me," explained Bertha. "I'm paid to do like she says. If you know what's good for you, you will too."

Small Shadow nodded. He would obey both Mrs.

Hicks and Dan'l. They were his friends, and he would please them in every way he could.

Immediately after supper, Dan'l went back to his office. He enjoyed a pipe after his meal, and Mrs. Hicks would not permit smoking in her house. Small Shadow went with him.

"Tomorrow I will empty out all your spittoons," he promised, looking at the three basins on the floor. He was surprised that they had not overflowed since yesterday.

"What for?" Dan'l began stuffing tobacco into the bowl of his corncob pipe.

"They're about to run over."

"Lots of room yet," said Dan'l mildly. "I say, they'll hold the juice from a lot of chaws yet. Besides, tomorrow's the day the Methodist ladies are fixing to sew. You'll have to stay home and try on your new clothes."

Small Shadow thought of Mrs. Gadsby and the expression on her face when she learned he had no underwear. Then he remembered the strange word he had meant to ask Dan'l about.

"What does contaminated mean?"

"Means tainted. Sometimes poisoned." Dan'l struck a match, holding the flame to his pipe. "You ever hear of a well that had a dead cat in it, Shad? That's contaminated water."

"Not a well," objected Small Shadow thoughtfully. "Not water. A house."

"Reckon it's the same idea," Dan'l began patiently, then broke off to look at him sharply. "Where'd you hear that word, anyway?"

"Mrs. Hicks said it."

"Oh." Dan'l relaxed. "If Old Lady Hicks said it, it's all right. She was probably talking about spoiled butter or such like. Nothing to fret yourself about."

Small Shadow did not correct him, but his mind was busy with the problem. Mrs. Hicks said her house was already contaminated. That meant it must contain something bad, and the other ladies didn't want it in their houses. He wondered what it could be.

Promptly at nine o'clock the next morning, the ladies began arriving at the front door. There were twelve of them, and they came loaded down with baskets, some of which contained food for the midday meal, while others held sewing supplies.

Mrs. Hicks introduced Small Shadow to each one as she arrived. In the beginning he smiled as he looked up into the curious, probing faces, but when he realized no one was smiling back, he stopped. Obviously Tom Smith had been wrong on this point. He said that whites smiled on greeting a stranger, but these ladies did not smile. They only stared, so Small Shadow stared back. Most of them had comments to make.

"Scrawny little thing, ain't he?"

42

"I just didn't believe it, not till I seen it with my own eyes."

"I see the Baptists haven't got into their barrel for shoes. Maybe it was all talk, and they don't have none."

"How old do you reckon he is, Mrs. Hicks?"

"Why don't you ask him yourself? Shad's got a tongue." Mrs. Hicks's voice snapped like a breaking stick. Shad saw that angry spots of red were glowing in her sallow cheeks.

"I have eleven summers." Small Shadow spoke to Mrs. Hicks since the question had been addressed to her. He knew his age. The priest who came to the agency once a month had told the boys how old they were. It was in their baptism records. In a little over a year, he would be a man.

"Now you know," said Mrs. Hicks, glaring at the one who had asked about his age.

"Well, let's get to work," said Dulcy Gadsby briskly. "We've lots to do. We want to show those Baptists what we can turn out when we've a mind to."

In the sitting room they began spreading out lengths of material on the center table, and Small Shadow's eyes grew round with wonder. There were figured percales and plain, and a great deal of heavy white cloth that Mrs. Gadsby pronounced suitable for underwear. Not all of the material was new. Many of the pieces had been salvaged from worn-out garments, but they had been washed, pressed flat, and the thin areas cut away. They would be just as good as new according to the ladies who had brought them.

Mrs. Flint, the one who had furnished something called a pattern, made a great to-do about it. It had fitted her boys, but of course they were huskier. It would be safer to take measurements before they cut into good material. From her sewing basket she produced a long strip of cloth with numbers printed on it, and presented it to Mrs. Hicks.

"You do it," she ordered.

With snapping eyes and tightly closed lips, Mrs. Hicks proceeded to measure Small Shadow. She held the strip around his chest and waist, across his shoulders and down his pants' leg, calling out numbers in a brittle voice. Small Shadow stood patiently, wondering what it was all about, but not daring to ask.

When she had finished, each lady seized one of the pieces of cloth and spread it out on a section of Mrs. Hicks's clean rag rug. Then she dropped to her knees on the floor and began studying it intently before attacking it with the scissors from her sewing basket.

The room, which had been humming with conversation since their arrival, grew silent as they concentrated. In this quiet Mrs. Hicks's voice sounded loud.

"Why don't you go in the kitchen, Shad, and wait with Bertha?" She did not sound angry any more, and she even managed a small smile. "We'll call you when somebody needs a fitting."

Small Shadow left willingly. The smell of so many whites in a single room was making his stomach churn. Bertha was poor company, since she seldom talked, but she was preferable to the ladies of the Missionary Society. He had suddenly realized that no one had spoken to him, only about him. It was as though he were a rock or a tree, without ears to hear or a tongue of his own. He wondered if Mrs. Hicks had noticed.

Since today was Saturday, Bertha was mixing bread. She looked up briefly as he entered; then her eyes turned back to the white dough she was knead-ing.

"They must be cutting out," she said after a minute. "You can always tell. Quiet as death, they are, while cutting out is going on. Feared to make a mistake."

Small Shadow nodded.

"Bertha, what's contaminated about this house?" he asked.

"You smell something?" She sniffed air through her long nose, turning her head from side to side. "I don't smell nothing. It's clean as an alder whistle."

"Can you always smell it if it's contaminated?"

"Mostly."

Small Shadow sniffed, too. He got up and walked about the kitchen, sniffing as he went. It smelled of baking pies and bread dough and the chicken she was frying for the midday meal. Those couldn't be contaminated.

He hadn't smelled anything but the ladies in the other room. He wondered when the contamination had taken place and if it would begin to smell before long.

At length Mrs. Hicks summoned him to the sitting room for a fitting. Garments had been cut out and were basted together with long stitches. He tried on two shirts and a coat; then Mrs. Hicks sent him into the parlor to put on two pairs of basted-up pants, one after the other. He had to return holding them up about his waist, for there were no buttons or suspenders. To his relief, no one suggested that he try on the underwear.

Mrs. Hicks did all the fitting, putting pins in seams to make them wider or narrower, lifting shoulders, pinning darts. Whoever had made the garment stood by, giving orders about moving pins this way or that. Mrs. Hicks obeyed silently, but Small Shadow could tell that she was still angry.

As he stood there patiently, his eyes inspected the circle of intent faces. The ladies looked very much alike, although some were tall and others short, some fat and others scrawny. They all wore long printed dresses, covered by white aprons. It was hard to tell them apart.

At noon, the ladies filled the places at the long

table in the dining room, and the regular boarders ate in the kitchen. Small Shadow was happy to see Dan'l and wished that he could return to town with him.

"They'll need you some more," Dan'l reminded him. "You can't have new clothes without suffering for them."

"Fine feathers never made fine birds," declared Jacob Riley.

Dan'l put down his fork and looked at him gleefully.

"You're slipping, Jacob. That ain't the Scriptures. I say, it's Ben Franklin or somebody or other—not the Bible at all."

"It come from a pious man, nevertheless," insisted Jacob, but his face reddened with embarrassment.

When everyone had eaten and returned to work, Bertha attacked the gigantic pile of dishes.

"I could wipe them if you want," suggested Small Shadow. It was better to do something than just sit. Ordinarily dishes were squaw's work, but since his mother's death the job had fallen to him at home. Of course, he didn't have to do them every day, only when they were too dirty to use again.

"Don't mind if you do," accepted Bertha promptly. "My corns is killing me. You're lucky, in a way, not to wear shoes."

"But I'm going to get some," he reminded her. "If the Baptist ladies remember."

"They will," she promised. "Us Baptists keep our

word. We go about our work quiet-like and don't make a big to-do about it, that's all."

In the middle of the afternoon, Small Shadow was called back for his final fitting. This time the seams were sturdily sewed, and there remained only hems and buttonholes.

Besides the underwear, which felt rough and scratchy, there were several calico shirts and three pairs of outside pants. Two of these were durable cotton, but one was of serviceable brown wool for Sundays.

Best of all, there was a coat. Someone said it had been made from parts of a blanket, but it was warm and comfortable. There were two pockets and a collar that could be turned up around his neck and didn't have to be held in place with one hand.

The ladies approved, too, and kept congratulating the one who had made it, whom they called Zelda Pugh. Small Shadow recognized the last name. She must be the wife of the man who owned the tannery just outside of town. He looked at her respectfully. She was short and plump, with black hair, and her face was flushed pink with all the praise the ladies were giving her.

"About here, Zelda?" asked Mrs. Hicks, bending over to insert a pin to mark the position of the hem.

Mrs. Pugh said that was just right, but when it came time to mark the closing at the front, she wasn't so easily pleased. First Mrs. Hicks marked the button-holes too loose; then they were too tight.

"I'll do it myself," declared Mrs. Pugh, jumping to her feet.

There was a great silence as she hurried across the room and took the pincushion from Mrs. Hicks. She was only a little taller than Small Shadow, and as she bent over, straightening the two coat fronts and bringing them together, he looked down at the straight white part in her hair. She hardly seemed aware of him, only of the splendid coat, and as she worked on, putting pins carefully in place, then standing back to observe the effect, the ladies watched.

At last she was finished, and she lifted her head to look into the face of the one who would wear her masterpiece. Small Shadow was pleased with the coat. He smiled his thanks, and Zelda Pugh smiled back. Then she patted him on the shoulder.

The ladies gasped. It made a small hissing sound in the quiet room, and Mrs. Pugh was suddenly aware of what she had done. The smile faded from her face, and she whirled around. All the ladies were looking at her.

"No need to stare like that," she declared defensively. "He didn't bite, and he didn't contaminate me. He's just a little boy. And I think we've all been acting like a flock of silly geese."

Without comment, Mrs. Hicks stepped forward and began shifting the pins so that Small Shadow could get out of the coat.

He hardly noticed. Now he knew what had contaminated Mrs. Hicks's house. Mrs. Pugh had made it very clear. It was his own presence. He was the contaminator.

Four

❦

"You'll have to leave off spading for a while, Shad," called Mrs. Hicks from the back porch. "I just used the last of the vanilla in the devil's food, and I'll need more for the whipped cream. Run down to Onnie Hatcher's and fetch me a bottle."

Shad—he never thought of himself as Small Shadow any more—thrust the blade deep in the soil and left it there. He didn't like to spade, but he'd rather do it than venture downtown by himself.

In the month he had spent in Evansdale, he had found there was little he could do for Dan'l Foster, but Mrs. Hicks more than made up for it. He split and carried wood, pumped buckets of water for the weekly washing, and now she had set him the task of preparing the soil for a vegetable garden.

Mrs. Hicks liked to see people work. The sight brought an approving glint to her gray eyes and a slight relaxing of her tight lips. She never said thank you or offered praise, but he had overheard her boasting of his industry to both Mrs. Gadsby and Mrs. Clifford. Shad was a real help around the place, a hard worker, and as neat as a pin. You'd never know, except for his color, that he was straight off the reservation.

"Now watch that you don't drop the bottle on the way back," she admonished, thrusting a coin into his hand. "Vanilla comes high. Onnie charges two bits for it, and twenty-five cents don't grow on trees."

"Yes, ma'am. I'll be careful."

"And hurry right back to finish," she shouted after him. "I figure to plant seeds tomorrow. Ground's just right for it."

Shad walked a little faster. He crossed the street and cut across the courthouse block, headed for Main Street.

Spring was advancing into Evansdale a little farther each day. The buds on the Hanging Tree had burst open, showing small green leaves. Two robins on one of its limbs were discussing the best location for a nest. The grass, under Shad's shabby, patched shoes from the Baptist missionary barrel, had grown taller since yesterday, and the April sun felt pleasantly warm on the new shirt sewed by the Methodist ladies. He crossed Main Street, stepping aside for a cow that had strayed from someone's barnyard and was now intent on the greener grass of the courthouse square.

All the time he kept hoping that Dan'l was in his office and would walk with him to Onnie Hatcher's store. Shad had never before come downtown without Dan'l's reassuring presence, and he felt uncomfortable.

Dan'l's office door was shut this morning, and when he opened it, the closed-up, musty smell of winter rushed out to greet him. Shad wrinkled his nose in distaste. The room should be given a good airing, the way women air out blankets and robes. Dan'l was not there, so he closed the door and forced himself to continue on down the block.

At least the street was deserted this morning, which was some comfort. He would have to face only the critical eyes of the storekeeper.

Living in Evansdale had not been the adventure Shad had expected. He wished he had never come. Since he had learned that the ladies thought he was contaminated, he had tried to stay away from them. He knew now that was the reason Mrs. Hicks had done the measuring and fitting. The others didn't want to touch him. They thought the contamination would rub off on their hands. But Mrs. Hicks didn't think so, so he stayed at home, carrying out her endless jobs. When callers stopped by, he went to another room or outside, taking his contamination as far away as possible.

Sometimes Dan'l insisted that Shad accompany him downtown. He said a boy couldn't be expected to work all the time. He always introduced Shad to his friends, but they never offered to shake hands as they would have done with Tom Smith or the older men on the reservation. Shad was careful not to smile, and he never spoke. Like the ladies, the men stared at him curiously, and sometimes their eyes said he was an unwanted intruder in their midst. But they never put their thoughts into words. Maybe they were afraid to. Dan'l usually had a protective arm around Shad's shoulders, and Tom Smith said that Dan'l could lick his weight in wildcats.

Shad wished again that Dan'l were here. It was scary venturing down the street alone. He peered through the window of the barbershop as he went by. The single chair was occupied, but it wouldn't be Dan'l beneath the foaming lather and the sheet. Dan'l had been shaved yesterday, and he wouldn't return to the barbershop until the end of the week.

Onnie Hatcher's General Store was the last building on the block, and Shad took a deep breath before he forced himself to enter. Before he had come to live in Evansdale, the store had seemed a wondrous place. It smelled of coffee and bacon, licorice candy and coal oil, pickles and sorghum molasses. The shelves were crowded with bolts of cloth and bottles of ointment and tonics, and you had to step around barrels of flour and sugar, nails, and chicken feed.

But the proprietor had made it quite plain that Shad was unwelcome. Even when he was in Dan'l's company, Mr. Hatcher never removed his eyes from the boy. He watched him carefully, answering Dan'l and the other customers absently, groping behind him on the shelves for orders as though he dared not look away.

To Shad's relief, he did not have to face Onnie Hatcher alone today. Rufus Gadsby was leaning across the counter, engaging the storekeeper in conversation.

Shad liked Mr. Gadsby better than any of the other whites. There were times when he seemed very friendly. He always talked to him, asking how he liked living at Old Lady Hicks's, and about his new clothes. It was as though he really wanted to know. But Shad didn't trust him. He didn't trust anyone but Mrs. Hicks and Dan'l.

Mr. Hatcher saw him first. He broke off in the middle of a sentence, and his tall frame seemed to stiffen while his eyes grew alertly watchful.

"You want something, boy?"

"Mrs. Hicks sent me for vanilla." Shad put the coin on the counter and stood back, waiting.

"Old Lady Hicks must be baking for tonight's doings." Rufus Gadsby nodded wisely. "What's she fixing to bring, Shad?"

"Something called devil's food." Shad had no idea what it was. He merely quoted her words. "The vanilla's for whipping cream."

"She makes a good devil's food cake, all right." Mr. Gadsby's voice was approving. "Not that it's as good as Dulcy's, but it'll do. Dulcy, now, she's bringing marble cake. Part white and part dark. That way every-body can have his ruthers."

The remark was made to the storekeeper, but he turned to include Shad, too.

Mr. Hatcher placed the vanilla bottle on the counter and snatched up the coin. His eyes said, "Go away. Leave my store." Shad turned to obey, but Rufe had a last question.

"You fixing to come to the doings with Dan'l and Mrs. Hicks?"

"I don't think so." Shad was surprised. The thought had not occurred to him, and no one had mentioned it. He knew the ladies were preparing a feast for that evening. It was in connection with something called a "lodge," but he had no idea what that was.

"They'll likely bring you. It's for all the families, and Dan'l tells everybody that's what you are." The round pink face beneath the wide-brimmed hat was smiling, but Shad did not notice. He only heard Onnie Hatcher's snort of disapproval before he hurried away.

The suggestion that he would be expected to attend tonight's gathering filled him with panic. Whatever it was, it would be crowded with people, white people with staring eyes and sneering faces—people who thought he was contaminated. If he were asked to go, he would make an excuse.

Mrs. Hicks, however, would not listen to excuses when he tried to make them at supper.

"Of course you'll go!" she declared indignantly. "It's my lodge, and my boarders count the same as family. 'Tisn't as though I had a living husband and young'uns of my own. You and Dan'l will come along at eight o'clock. Jacob, being Doc Riley's brother, will go with him, as is fit and proper."

Dan'l looked up from his plate, and the blue eyes beneath the bristling brows were thoughtful.

"Sounds like you don't want to go, Shad. I say, it sounds like you got something against the doings at the ladies' lodge."

"Maybe he's just smart," said Jacob Riley. "When the ladies finish setting out their table, there'll be no room left to squeeze in another dish. There'll be many a aching stomach tomorrow from them that practices gluttony tonight."

"Pshaw, Jacob. You talk like it was a full meal," objected Mrs. Hicks. "It's just cake and coffee."

Nothing more was said about Shad staying home. Everyone seemed to take it for granted that he would go. Mrs. Hicks hurried them through supper, explaining there would be no pie tonight since there would be all that cake later on. Then she whisked off the apron that covered her best dress, and carrying a three-layered devil's food cake, thickly coated with whipped cream, she departed.

Jacob Riley left, too, for the home of his brother and sister-in-law whose guest he would be for the evening.

"Might as well go down to the office and wait," said Dan'l. "I can smoke my pipe there. Come along, Shad."

Bertha was preparing to wash the dishes as they paused in the kitchen for their coats. She filled the pan from the teakettle on the stove and dropped in plates and cups with a ruthlessness she never would have dared in Mrs. Hicks's presence. Shad noticed that her heavy features looked sullen and resentful.

"Are you coming to the lodge later on, Bertha?" he asked.

"Why'd I want to go there?" She sounded so cross that Shad stared in surprise. Then Dan'l was urging him outside into the gathering twilight.

"Bertha don't belong to the lodge, Shad," he explained, once the door was closed behind them. "Not everybody does. The ladies vote on who they want to join."

"We don't belong either."

"Old Lady Hicks counts us as family since we pay board. Bertha gets paid for working, which makes it some different."

Shad wished that he and Bertha could change places for the evening. He didn't want to go, and somehow he sensed that she did. But at least he had learned one thing. Whites were not all equal just because their skin color was the same.

As they walked, Dan'l explained about the lodge. It was an organization of people who liked each other and who met at appointed times. The men had their own lodge, but the party they were to attend was given by the ladies. Mrs. Hicks had left early to help get ready. Then the doors would be opened to receive their guests.

"There'll be a lot of folks there," he concluded. "Most of them you already know, at least by sight. You got to face them, Shad, and speak up. Speaking up's important. I say, you can't bury your head like an ostrich just because some folks are petty and bigoted. How can they get to know you if you don't give them a chance?"

Shad hung his head. He hadn't realized that Dan'l had noticed how closely he had been staying at home.

"To make a friend you got to be a friend," explained Dan'l when it was clear that Shad had nothing to say. "You got to keep smiling, even when you don't feel like it. And it don't hurt to give a compliment, neither, particularly to somebody you think don't care for you much. I say, you can catch more flies with molasses than with vinegar."

"I'll try," Shad promised, but he didn't have much hope for success. He had tried smiling at the sewing bee, and no one had smiled back.

When they arrived, they found that Rufe Gadsby was already occupying Dan'l's office. He had lighted the lamp and was sitting tilted back in one of the chairs, his feet propped on the cold stove.

"Evening," he called.

"Evening, Rufe," answered Dan'l.

For a moment Shad hesitated. Always before he had let Dan'l answer for them both. Now he spoke up bravely.

"Evening, Mr. Gadsby."

For a moment the round pink face beneath its ring of white curls turned to him in surprise. Then Rufus Gadsby smiled widely.

"See, I told you you'd be coming to the doings," he pointed out. "And here you are."

Shad felt himself grow warm with pleasure. Maybe Dan'l was right. Smiling wasn't enough. You had to speak as well. He sat down in one of the chairs, and whenever he caught Rufus Gadsby's eye, he smiled. To his delight, the smile was always returned.

Before long they were joined by Doc Riley and Jacob, and Shad tried it again.

"Evening, Doc Riley," he called as soon as they opened the door.

"Evening, Shad," said Doc Riley. He seemed a little surprised, but he smiled as he spoke. Once again Shad was delighted.

"This your first time at the ladies' doings, I reckon," Doc said jovially, taking the chair next to Shad's. "So let me give you a piece of advice. If you try to sample every one of them cakes, even if it's just a sliver, you be sure to ask Mrs. Hicks for some baking soda before you go to bed. Take it in a little water."

Everyone laughed, and the conversation turned to

other matters. Shad didn't try to enter in. He didn't need to. He felt included, and he was happier than he had been since the night of his arrival. Dan'l's formula had worked twice. There was no reason why it shouldn't again.

At last someone announced that it was five minutes to eight and time to leave. Dan'l blew out the lamp, and they all filed out into the street.

It was very dark, for clouds had swept in to cover the sky. The only light came from above and below the swinging doors of the Golden Bird Saloon next door. Shad, who brought up the rear, could hear voices inside, and the sound of laughter, but as they walked on, the noises faded away.

"Someday there'll be lights on this street." Rufe Gadsby's voice came from the shadows ahead. "We'll have real lights on the corners, same as they have in big cities. I'll bet you a cooky on that."

"Streetlights is the signposts of the devil." That was Jacob Riley's voice. "What call we got for lights? Decent folks should keep behind doors at nighttime."

"And miss all them good cakes the ladies baked for us?" That had to be Doc Riley, Shad decided. Almost everyone else in Evansdale ignored most of Jacob's remarks.

"Whoa," called Dan'l, who was in the lead. "We're at the corner. Turn left."

The lodge hall was on a side street near the edge of town. Echo Creek wound its way through a vacant field to their right, and straight ahead was the campground, site of the Fourth of July celebrations. The building itself was of a single story. It looked like a residence, with a narrow porch running across the front and a centered door, flanked by windows. Only a little light filtered through the dark muslin curtains, but there was enough to see that the porch was crowded with men and children.

"We're early," said Dan'l. "I say, I should have finished my pipe after all."

"We're just in time," corrected Rufe. "They're opening the doors."

There was a mad rush as those already on the porch began pushing to get inside. While they awaited their own turn, Shad moved ahead to stand by Dan'l. Even though things were going well, he felt safer that way.

"They must have started the line right off." Rufus Gadsby was disappointed. "No other reason to take so long. They're moving slower than molasses in January."

"Don't worry, Rufe. There'll be plenty. The cake won't run out before you get there," Doc assured him.

It was some time before they were able to reach the open doorway, and Shad was unprepared for the delicious aromas that filled the room. Above all was the smell of coffee, prepared in a washboiler on the wood stove in one corner. Running it a close second were the blendings of more cakes than he had ever seen gathered at one time. They stretched from one end to the other of a long trestle table set up on wooden sawhorses, and while slices had been cut from several, more than enough remained for second and third helpings for everyone. There were chocolate cakes with white frosting, chocolate cakes with chocolate frosting, white cakes and yellow cakes, spice cakes and devil's food, angel food and sponge cake, marble cake and pound cake, and others that Shad could not identify.

Behind the table stood some of the ladies, urging their guests to sample one or another, or several, of the delicacies. Their smiles were constant, and while no one spoke to Shad directly, there was no time for the smiles to fade between greeting Dan'l and Rufe Gadsby. Shad took some of whatever Dan'l chose, and soon his heavy crockery plate was heaped high.

At the end of the line, however, it was different. The dispensing of coffee was too serious for smiles. Mrs. Evans, wife of the editor of the *Valley Sentinel*, presided over a huge granite coffeepot, filling the heavy cups and urging everyone to help himself to sugar and cream. Mrs. Hatcher was her assistant, re-filling the pot as it was emptied from the washboiler on the stove.

Mrs. Evans filled Dan'l's cup and looked sternly at Shad.

"Coffee?"

"Yes, please." He liked coffee. Everyone on the reservation did, especially when there was plenty of sugar in it.

"Coffee's not good for growing boys. It stunts their growth." She frowned, but tilted the granite pot, which was getting low.

Shad was embarrassed. If she hadn't wanted him to have coffee, she shouldn't have asked. His eyes fell on Mrs. Hatcher, waiting to refill the coffeepot as soon as it was emptied. Mrs. Hatcher looked definitely disapproving. Like her husband, the storekeeper, she obviously had no fondness for Indians. He decided to try Dan'l's advice about complimenting someone who didn't like you.

"That's a real pretty pin you've got on, Mrs. Hatcher," he told her politely, nodding toward the gold brooch on her tatted lace collar.

Mrs. Hatcher's hand went protectively to her throat, covering the pin. She did not answer, nor did the compliment seem to soften her dislike. She stared at him suspiciously, and when Mrs. Evans handed her the now empty coffeepot, she took it and hurried back to the stove without saying a word.

Shad added three spoonfuls of sugar to his coffee and carried his plate and cup to where Dan'l was sitting in the row of chairs that lined the room. Rufus Gadsby joined them there.

"Hope you didn't take none of the sponge cake," he said, sitting down and adjusting his heaped plate to his knee. "That's what Mrs. Evans made, and she's the worst cook in town. Of course some of the others brung sponge cake, too, but it's flying in the face of providence to take a chance. Sure as shooting, the one you picked would be Mrs. Evans's."

Shad was too busy eating to listen to their conversation. He had four kinds of cake on his plate, and he had never tasted anything so good. Each one he sampled seemed even better than the one before. He finished them off, hoping that Dan'l would suggest going back for seconds.

Suddenly from across the room there came a high-pitched shriek. A second later a woman's voice began shouting, "Thief! Thief! Robber!"

"What in tarnation do you suppose has happened?" Rufe Gadsby's voice quivered with excitement. "Who is that yelling anyway, Dan'l?"

Dan'l didn't know. The sounds were coming from behind the serving table that was hidden from their view by those who had gone back to refill their plates.

From the end where the coffee was served, Mrs. Hatcher now burst forth, pushing aside all who were in her way. Her face was flushed and angry as she stood there, her glance traveling along the line of chairs against the wall. It stopped when it came to Dan'l, Rufe, and Shad, sitting openmouthed with surprise, and she advanced upon them angrily.

"Thief!" she screamed, her voice echoing against the walls of the square room. "Robber! I don't know how you did it, but you give me back my solid gold brooch!"

At first Shad did not know she was speaking to him. Until she stopped directly before his chair, hand outstretched, angry eyes upon his face, he had no idea that she was accusing him. Then he saw that the gold pin, which he had admired, was missing from her collar.

He felt himself grow cold, and all that cake, which had tasted so good before, began to churn in his stomach.

"I didn't take your pin, Mrs. Hatcher." His lips had grown so stiff that he could hardly form the words.

"Now hold on a minute." Dan'l raised his voice. "What's all this about a brooch?"

"He stole it, that's what," she insisted, her finger pointing straight at Shad. "Wasn't very smart about it, neither, or he wouldn't have said to my face that he liked it. Mrs. Evans heard him, too. You can ask her if you want. Then, when my back was turned, he had it off my collar some way and into his pocket. Look, and you'll find it there."

"But he already said he didn't take it," Dan'l argued quietly. "And if he said he didn't, he didn't. I say, Shad's no liar."

The room had grown very still, and Shad was unpleasantly aware that everyone was looking at him. He wished there were some way he could get out of here, away from those rows of staring, unfriendly eyes. No one would believe he hadn't taken the brooch, no one but Dan'l.

"Of course, he's a liar. All Injuns lie," cried Mrs. Hatcher indignantly. "They lie and they got sticky fingers, too. The minute you turn your back, they steal you blind. The things Onnie's had stolen when the Injuns are in town you'd never believe."

"There's a few that do, but there's more that don't," pointed out Dan'l calmly. "The same can be said for white people. I say, I could name several in this very room that never passes Onnie's pickle barrel without dipping in or are above helping themselves to an apple neither. You don't call that stealing?"

"Well, yes," she admitted reluctantly. "But when Onnie catches them, he just adds the price to their bill. Injuns from the reservation don't run bills."

"Have you looked around for your brooch, Mrs. Hatcher?" asked Rufe Gadsby anxiously. "It could easily have dropped off on the floor and rolled."

"Of course I looked." Her voice was snappish. "Me and Mrs. Evans both. It was on my collar when he went through the line. That's when he said how pretty it was. I had a feeling even then, so I felt to make sure it was there. Then when I felt again, it was gone. Somebody in this room took it, and it has to be him. The rest of the folks are good lodge members and their kin. It couldn't be one of them."

The room had been very quiet. Now it began to buzz with low remarks as people turned to comment to each other. It was like the sound of bees around their hive.

From behind the serving table came a new commotion, and a moment later Mrs. Hicks pushed through the crowd. Angry red splotches marked her sallow cheeks, and her gray eyes snapped as she strode across the room.

Shad watched her come, and he wished more than ever that he could get away. Mrs. Hicks was upset. More than once she had expressed her feelings about liars and thieves. Probably she was going to tell him what she thought of him in front of everyone.

But Mrs. Hicks was not looking at him. Her eyes were on Mrs. Hatcher, and as she drew near, she extended her hand. In her fingers was an object too small to recognize.

"Here's your precious brooch, Alma Hatcher," she announced loudly. "Mrs. Evans poured it out with the last cup of coffee. You must have loosened the clasp when you felt to make sure it was there, and it fell in the pot without your noticing."

"Oh," said Mrs. Hatcher weakly. She took the brooch from Mrs. Hicks.

"As for the rest of you," declared Mrs. Hicks, turning so that her scornful gaze moved around the lines of openmouthed spectators, "Dan'l could say this a lot better than me, but it's on my tongue, and it's got to come out. You should be ashamed, every last one of you, putting the blame on somebody just because it's easy and it saves your own consciences. Some of you've got reason not to like Injuns. Maybe you or your folks had bad trouble with them crossing the plains. But there's no call to hold it against Shad. He wasn't one that swung a tomahawk. He wasn't even born yet. He can't help the color of his skin, and anyway what counts is what's underneath. Inside he's just the same as you are."

"I couldn't have said it better, Mrs. Hicks," declared Dan'l admiringly. He reached over and pulled Shad to his feet, going to stand behind her on the floor. "And the way I see it, those that feel it was a shame to put him to all this mortifying should tell him so."

"My sentiments exactly," cried Rufe Gadsby as he joined them.

"And mine," echoed Doc Riley, standing up.

"He who is without sin, let him cast the first stone," declared Jacob, taking a firm stand beside his brother.

The hard lump in Shad's stomach melted as the citizens of Evansdale began crowding around, anxious to prove it had been a mistake. His hand tingled and grew numb as one after another they took turns in shaking it. His face ached from smiling, but he didn't care. Everyone smiled back, and he knew that many of them meant it. Best of all, their touch proved that he was no longer contaminated.

Five

Shad looked up from the bucket he was filling at the
pump, and the stream of water trickled to a stop as he
forgot to raise and lower the handle. There they were
again! Every morning when he filled the water buckets for Mrs. Hicks, he saw them. At this same hour
two boys walked down Washington Street, cut across
the courthouse yard, and then turned south. They
never came near enough for him to distinguish their
features, and he didn't know who they were, but they
were close to his own age. Whenever he saw them, a
feeling of loneliness welled up inside him and stayed
there a long time.

Since that evening at the ladies' lodge, Shad was no
longer afraid to walk downtown by himself. Most of
the men, and some of the women, nodded and spoke
to him as he passed by. Some even called him by
name. It was gratifying, but he soon realized it wasn't
enough. They were all his elders, and it was lonely
living in a world of grownups. He needed someone
his own age to talk with, perhaps to play a game or
do something that was fun. Of course, he could never
find anyone to replace his old friends on the reserva-

tion. There would never be another Ned or Chicken, Dave or Mose in Evansdale, but he wished he knew someone who wasn't old.

For a time he considered telling Dan'l Foster about it. Dan'l might understand. But then he would feel guilty because he hadn't thought of it himself, and Shad wouldn't want that. It would be better if he just made friends by himself.

The problem was, how could he get to know some of the boys? They were seldom downtown in the evenings when he returned with Dan'l, or if they were, they were always in laughing, busy groups of their own. He watched them secretly at church, which he dutifully attended with Mrs. Hicks each Sunday, and sometimes he observed them watching him, too. But afterward they were escorted home immediately by their parents, probably to change out of their best clothes. Mrs. Hicks hurried him home for the same purpose, and the rest of the day was spent quietly. The Lord did not approve of work or roisterous behavior on His day.

Shad had decided that he would have to make his own opportunity. He concentrated on the two boys who were now crossing the courthouse yard. They were followed by a small group of girls, headed in the same direction, but Shad wasn't interested in them. Girls weren't of much use until you were grown and needed someone to keep house and work for you. He knew that all the children would disappear for the whole day and not return until late afternoon. At that time, they were usually in a hurry. Probably they had to do similar chores to those he himself performed each morning.

He suddenly noticed that the water had stopped, and he had to prime the pump and start all over. When the bucket was full, he carried it inside and put it on the table.

"Every morning I see two boys come down the street," he told Bertha, who was alone in the kitchen. "Do you know who they are?"

"Likely a couple of the Flint young'uns on their way to school," she answered.

"Do they go every day?"

"Not on Saturday or Sunday. Other days they do. But you won't see them long. School will be out soon. Runs from the middle of October till the middle of April. Rest of the year their folks need them to help with the work."

He understood about that. His father's reservation land was too far from the agency for Shad to attend school, but those who lived close by always missed school whenever there were chores to be done.

"What time is school out in the afternoon?"

"Four-thirty or thereabouts." She frowned. "You jabber too much. Get on with your work."

Shad obeyed meekly. Bertha had told him all he needed to know. He thought about the problem while his ax cut lengths of soft fir into kindling. Dan'l had

72

said that to make a friend you had to be one, and that was good advice. He must smile and speak first, and to do so, he would have to seek out the boys where they were, at school. And he must do it soon.

His chores for Mrs. Hicks occupied the entire morning, but after the midday meal he always went downtown with Dan'l. When the lawyer was busy, Rufe Gadsby kept him company.

Once Rufe had been a prosperous farmer, but now he had sold his farm and moved into town, where he lived with his wife and his orphaned granddaughter, Tine. Nowadays, Rufe had nothing to do but occupy himself with the affairs of other townspeople, and he was always glad for Shad's company.

Today all three of them gathered in Dan'l's office. It had begun raining at noon, and they had drawn their chairs close around the stove. Dan'l and Rufe talked, but Shad hardly listened. He was too busy with his plan for meeting some of the boys. He had decided that it must be done this afternoon.

"Feels more like February than April," complained Rufe, aiming an expert stream at the nearest spittoon. "That's what Dulcy said at dinner today. 'Rufe,' she said, 'it feels exactly like February. Hope it don't drop down to a freeze at night and spoil the crops.'"

"What time is it?" asked Shad.

Dan'l looked at him in surprise as he drew a large gold watch from his vest pocket.

"This time it's three o'clock. What's so important

about the time, Shad? I say, you've been asking me the time every half hour the whole afternoon."

"You going somewheres?" demanded Rufe. "Or expecting somebody?"

"I'm going for a walk." Shad stood up and reached for his coat on the wall. It was too early, but he couldn't make himself sit there any longer.

"On a day like this?" Rufe was scandalized. "Have you taken leave of your wits?"

"Let him go," advised Dan'l mildly. "He's got something on his mind. I say, I've known that ever since dinner. And it's something he's got to work out by himself."

Shad looked at him gratefully. Dan'l always understood. He understood everything except Shad's need for a friend his own age.

Once outside, he began to have doubts. Bertha said school lasted until four-thirty. He couldn't stand in the rain for an hour and a half, waiting for the boys. But he couldn't sit quietly in Dan'l's office, either. His nerves were quivering like a bowstring after an arrow. Maybe he'd just walk down and look at the outside of the school, then return. It would help pass the time.

He turned south, and the wind blew the rain into his face, so that he had to bow his head. Across the street, the budding branches of the Hanging Tree swayed and twisted. He forced himself to go on. Any day now school might be over for the year. When the boys scattered to work for their fathers, he might never find them. This could be his last chance.

The school was on the last block of Main Street, just beyond the Baptist Church and across the road from Rufe Gadsby's neat white house. The yard surrounding it was an expanse of mud. Only a few clumps of sturdy grass had withstood the pounding feet of the students. There was a well at the side and a stack of firewood for the heating stove.

As Shad approached, a boy opened the door and stepped out into the rain, headed for the woodpile. He was muffled in a coat, with a knit cap pulled down over his ears, so Shad could not recognize his features. He wouldn't know the boy anyway, he told himself, and besides it didn't matter. It was as though that providence Mrs. Hicks was always talking about had sent the stranger outside at the moment Shad needed him. He hurried forward eagerly.

The boy saw him coming and stopped. In the space between his turned-up collar and the knitted cap, hazel eyes stared hard with suspicion.

"Hello," said Shad. When the boy did not answer, he continued. "Did you come for wood? I'll help you carry it."

"You keep your dirty hands off this wood," ordered the boy quickly.

The collar fell open as he spoke, and Shad's heart stopped for a moment. He did recognize this boy after all. He had seen him in church, sitting with Mr. and

Mrs. Hatcher. He was their son, and his name was Walter.

"What are you doing on the school grounds, anyway?" demanded Walter angrily. "They're for whites, not dirty redskins. Why don't you go back to the reservation? Nobody wants you here."

"I live with Dan'l Foster," Shad reminded him. He would have turned and left, but he knew instinctively that Walter Hatcher would boast to the others that he had made an Indian run just by talking. Shad didn't want that.

"You think Dan'l Foster really wants you?" taunted Walter. "He don't. My pa says if Dan'l Foster had any gumption, he'd have sent you packing long ago. Dan'l Foster's just like an old woman, too tenderhearted to—"

Shad didn't wait to hear any more. He hit Walter with all the strength in his right arm. The white boy staggered, his feet slipped on the muddy ground, and he sprawled on his back. Shad was on him in an instant, pinning him to the ground and battering with both fists.

"You take that back!" he demanded. "You take back what you said about Dan'l Foster. You take it back!"

Walter did not retract his words, but he began to yell. He was larger than Shad, but the flesh beneath his thick coat felt soft and yielding. He did not know how to protect himself. For a moment Shad hesitated.

This was not like the rough-and-tumble fights he used to enjoy with his friends. It was all one-sided, his side, and unfair.

Walter saw the opportunity, slid out from under, and got to his feet. He began to jab at Shad's head. His groping, pudgy fingers tried to poke at eyes, but Shad knew all about these tricks. He ducked away and hit back.

The next thing he knew, someone was pulling them apart. His coat collar was being held by a man who clutched Walter Hatcher with his other hand. The man was tall, red-faced, and very angry.

"What's all this about?" he demanded. "We heard you clear inside the school with the doors closed."

"He was trying to steal wood," said Walter, whimpering. "I caught him at it."

"That's a lie," denied Shad scornfully. "Why would I steal wood?"

"Because it isn't yours. Injuns always steal. It's in their blood. My pa says so," insisted Walter. "You should be glad I stopped him from stealing school property, Mr. Short."

"I don't think he was trying to take the wood, Mr. Short," said a girl's voice behind them. "I was looking out the window. The Indian boy just crossed the yard and said something to Walter, and then they began to fight. He didn't touch the wood."

Shad glanced over his shoulder. The yard was filled with children. They had followed the schoolmaster outside, and now they stood in the rain, watching. Some of the faces were serious, others grinning with enjoyment. He suddenly hated them all. He would never be friends with them. Never!

"You get back inside, all of you," ordered the schoolmaster. "Who gave you leave to stop your work? Walter, you go, too. I'll deal with you later. And you, young man"—he looked sternly at Shad—"I've got no authority over you. But you go back and tell Mr. Foster that you've been fighting on school grounds. Tell him to see me if he needs more particulars."

He loosened his grip, and Shad walked away. Behind him he could hear the voices of the children, discussing the excitement. Hatred burned deep within him, and he wondered how he could have ever wanted one of them for a friend.

Dan'l and Rufe were still sitting beside the stove when he returned. His new coat was caked with mud, and a bruise on his face was turning blue.

"What happened to you?" demanded Rufe in alarm. "Looks like you've been in a fight."

Shad nodded. "I walked past the school grounds. There was a boy outside. We had a fight."

"Know who he was?" asked Dan'l curiously.

"Walter Hatcher."

"Take off your coat and hang it close to the fire," said Dan'l. "A lot of that mud will brush off when it's dry. What started the fight?"

"He said something I didn't like," Shad told him reluctantly. "I started it."

Dan'l and Rufe exchanged glances. To his surprise they did not ask what Walter had said.

"Don't you give it no mind," said Rufe consolingly. "Onnie Hatcher's always shooting off his mouth, too, and his young'un's just like him."

"Sometimes it takes a good fight to clear the air," said Dan'l. "It was that way when I was a sprout, too. I'll explain it to Old Lady Hicks. There's times when boys just got to fight. I say, it's in their nature."

Six

※❖※

"How'd you like to have a job?" asked Dan'l. "Earn a little money for yourself?"

Shad had been sifting wood ashes for Mrs. Hicks, who needed them in her preparation of soft soap. He put down the wire sieve and stared up in amazement. No one had ever offered him a chance to earn money before.

"What you doing home this time of day, Dan'l Foster?" Mrs. Hicks had come around the corner of the house, carrying the huge copper kettle she used for soapmaking, but had arrived too late to hear the question.

"I come for Shad," Dan'l told her mildly. "Ralph Evans needs a boy at the *Valley Sentinel*. I figured it might be a chance for Shad to pick up a little chicken feed."

"Shad works for me mornings as you very well know," she reminded him severely.

"You got first call on his services, all right," agreed Dan'l. "And there's half a dozen boys in town Ralph can get if you really need him. But Abe Flint's oldest boy works there regular. I say, it would be nice for

Shad to get acquainted with somebody near his own age. It's not right for him to stick with the old folks all the time."

Shad looked back at the ashes. He wondered how Dan'l had arrived at such a conclusion. He had never told anyone the reason for his trip to the school, and no one had questioned him about it. Dan'l had taken Mrs. Hicks aside and explained about the muddy coat and the bruised cheek. She had told Bertha to sponge off the mud and had let the matter drop. A week ago Shad would have been delighted to meet some boys. Now he wanted to stay as far away from them as possible.

"There's something to that," Mrs. Hicks agreed thoughtfully. "The Flints is good folks, and their young'uns is well spoken. 'Twouldn't be like that ornery Walter Hatcher. What kind of job?"

"Don't rightly know. But Ralph seems hard put with the *Sentinel* coming out today. That young fellow he had working for him up and lit out this morning. Took the stage to Salem. The Flint boy can help, but Ralph needs somebody to take on the Flint boy's chores. Reckon he can get somebody else, though."

"He'll do no such thing," denied Mrs. Hicks fiercely. "It's high time somebody but me sees what a good, dependable worker Shad is. Me and Bertha can manage with the soap. We always have."

Shad heard her decision with mixed emotions. He would like to earn some money. Such an opportunity had never come to him before. But he wanted nothing to do with any strange white boy.

"Well, what you waiting for?" asked Mrs. Hicks impatiently. "I said you could go."

"Shall I change to my good pants?" He stood up reluctantly. He would have to go. Mrs. Hicks and Dan'l expected it of him. He must remember Tom Smith's advice about closing his ears to insults, no matter how hard it was to do.

"Better not," advised Dan'l. "You'll come home black as any ink pot, and Mrs. Hicks may not even let you in the house."

"There'll be plenty of hot water and soap." Mrs. Hicks frowned. "It'll be honest dirt that come from honest work."

As they walked to town, Shad tried to put the uneasy thoughts from his mind. He did his best to act pleased about the job because that was what Dan'l expected. He remembered what Tom Smith had said about the sounds of the huge machine that made black tracks on white paper and was glad that he had been warned.

The offices of the *Valley Sentinel* were on the first block of Main Street, next to Jackson's Harness Shop and across the street from Cosper's Livery Stable. The front door was flanked by two grimy windows, one displaying a heavy cardboard sign.

Shad tugged at Dan'l's coat. "What does that say?"

"It used to say, 'Job Printing Neatly Done,'" said

Dan'l scornfully, opening the door. "But it's got so fly-speckled and dirty, I'm not surprised you can't figure it out."

The huge black machine, which stood at the far end of the single room, had not yet been put to work. There was no loud, crashing noise, only a steady clicking, like someone shaking a handful of pebbles in a sack. Coming from the bright sunlight made it difficult to see, for inside they were in a world of semi-gloom. Shad wrinkled his nose at the strange odors, printer's ink, sour paste, and metallic grime. He could identify none of them.

"Morning, Mr. Foster." A boy, a few years older than Shad, stepped forward to greet them. He wore dirty jeans and a long apron that was so speckled with ink spots, it was hard to guess the original color. His face, too, was streaked with black, but he was smiling widely.

"Morning," said Dan'l. "You're one of Abe Flint's boys, aren't you? Let's see, you're—"

"I'm Frank. Frank Flint." He had not left off smiling, and his eyes were studying Shad. There was nothing critical in the smile, only friendliness. Shad felt the tight knot in his stomach begin to ease. Perhaps this would not be like his first encounter with a white boy after all. Then he reminded himself that it was too soon to tell. He must move cautiously.

"This is Shad," said Dan'l. "Ralph asked me to bring him over."

"I know," agreed Frank. "Mr. Evans is setting type right now, but he'll be through in a minute."

By now Shad had discovered the source of the clicking sound. The editor of the *Valley Sentinel* was gathering small bits of metal into a long stick. It did not look difficult, but he was concentrating hard and did not look up.

Shad had already met Ralph Evans on his evening excursions downtown. The editor was younger than Dan'l or Rufe and had thinning black hair carefully parted in the middle. His eyeballs looked too large for their sockets, for they protruded noticeably. He used very large words, many of which Shad had never heard. He wondered why Mr. Evans had offered him this job, and decided it was probably because Dan'l had asked him.

When Mr. Evans finished, he placed the column carefully on a stone-topped table and then crossed the room to greet them.

"I see you brought him," he observed. "It's a bad day to break in a new printer's devil. Lots to do with the *Sentinel* coming out. Frank will have to help me and supervise your boy at the same time. I don't want him at the cases today, Frank. It's too tricky. Do it yourself, and let him watch."

"Yes, sir," said Frank.

"Blast that Ed Wheeler, anyway," sputtered Mr. Evans angrily. "He was a good apprentice. But they're all alike. Can't trust them. Get to know a little about the business, and then they take off without a fare-thee-well."

"Didn't give a reason, I suppose?" asked Dan'l curiously.

"A weak one. Claimed he didn't like Mrs. Evans's cooking. He ate with us as part of his salary." He turned to Shad. "We need somebody two days a week, Thursday, when the *Sentinel* goes to press, and Wednesday, when we're getting ready. That's when Frank's been working. I'm promoting him to apprentice, and he'll quit school and stay on full time now. A couple of days is enough for a printer's devil. We'll see how you work out."

"How about wages, Ralph?" asked Dan'l. "I say, what you figure on paying Shad?"

The editor frowned. "He won't be much use at first. He'll have to be taught everything. Maybe twenty-five cents a day to start."

"That's mighty low, even for a beginner. How about fifty? You won't be boarding him. I say, he'll be eating at home."

"So does Frank. I'll pay him four dollars a week. If I pay a printer's devil another dollar, that brings up the overhead too much. I'll go thirty and not a penny more. And if he's no good, out he goes."

"He'll be good," Dan'l promised. He patted Shad on the shoulder, smiled at Frank, and returned to his office.

"There's not much for us to do while Mr. Evans

locks up the type," said Frank. "I can show you around and explain things. Did you bring an apron?"

Shad shook his head. He hadn't known an apron was needed.

"Mr. Wheeler left in such a hurry, he forgot his. You can wear that," suggested Frank.

The apron had a bib and covered Shad from his neck to his feet. It was nearly as soiled as the one Frank was wearing, but Shad was glad of the protection. Next week he would put on his reservation clothes. Mrs. Hicks would never approve of ink spots on the garments sewed by the Methodist ladies.

Mr. Evans was still busy with his type. He had imposed it on the stone-topped table, locked it in a case, and transferred it to the Washington press. Frank conducted Shad around the room, explaining rapidly as he went. The long central table was for folding papers once they had been printed. That would be one of Shad's jobs. He would also be required to wash the rollers of the press, keep the paste pots filled, the type dampened, carry rolls of paper, and return the half-pied type to the depleted cases that lined one wall.

"But you won't do that today," he concluded. "Mr. Evans wants you to watch me the first time. Mr. Wheeler, the man who left, says printer's devils, like us, aren't always expected to put type back in cases. Lots of times the printer wants to do it himself, to make sure it's right. But Mr. Evans doesn't like to put away type. He hates the job of tidying up."

Shad could well believe it. After the immaculate neatness of Mrs. Hicks's house, the *Valley Sentinel* was something of a shock. There were papers everywhere, papers in rolls, in stacks of assorted sizes and thicknesses, even small bits scattered here and there. At the far end was a desk, obviously used by the editor, for it was covered with more paper, and there were paste and ink pots and an assortment of quill pens stuck in a drinking glass. There was a trough, filled with water, under one window, and a basin for hand washing beside a grimy roller towel in the corner.

"Everybody quiet now!" Mr. Evans's reedy voice rose threateningly. "I am about to compose. I've made room for another story on the front page, and a follow-up on page two. The public needs to be told of the perfidy of a thankless apprentice who deserted his benefactor on press day."

Frank nodded. He drew Shad away from the type cases and toward the door.

"We'll wait outside," he whispered. "When Mr. Evans is composing a story, he doesn't want anybody around. He'll call us when he's through."

"It's nice of you to help me get started and explain everything," said Shad shyly when the door had closed behind them. Mrs. Hicks and Dan'l were right. Frank Flint was not like Walter Hatcher at all. If he thought Shad was a savage or a dirty redskin, he didn't show it. "I've never had a job before."

"This is my first one, too," Frank told him. "My brothers work in Pa's mill, but I wanted to do something on my own."

"Do you like it?"

"Parts of it. I don't like putting away type any more than Mr. Evans does. But after today, you'll be doing that."

"What is type?" Shad hadn't understood those bits of metal Frank had showed him at all, but he hadn't wanted to interrupt the explanation. "What's it for?"

"Why, it's type. You know, letters. Alphabet letters that make up words."

Shad shook his head. He still did not understand.

"You know your alphabet, don't you?" asked Frank, and when Shad shook his head, his dirty face grew long. "Then how can you work on a newspaper?"

"Can't I learn it?" asked Shad anxiously. "Can't you teach me?"

"I don't know," said Frank doubtfully. "It's hard. Haven't you ever been to school?"

Shad shook his head. It hadn't seemed important before, but now he wished he had talked his father into letting him go long enough to learn this thing called an alphabet.

Until last year, the Sisters of the Holy Name had done their best to conduct a boarding school on the reservation. It was situated near the agency, and when the surrounding land had been assigned to the Indians, the old and infirm had been given the closest plots. Lew Youngbuck was an able-bodied man, so his acreage was several miles distant. It was too far for Shad to make the round trip daily, and his father wanted him to live at home.

Besides, no one considered the school of real importance. Families who enrolled their children often withdrew them after a few weeks. By that time the nuns would have outfitted their students with new clothing. New pants and shirts and dresses kept a person warm and were a matter of prestige. But what would it avail a child to learn to read? Reading did not help plow a field or raise a crop. It did not make a better hunter or a fisherman. The tribal stories could not be found in books. They were told and retold by the old men. Learning to read and write was a waste of time, and due to the lack of students, the sisters had finally closed their doors.

"I'll try hard," pleaded Shad. "Maybe I can learn. Nobody's ever given me a chance at a job before. If you'll help me, I promise to work at it."

Frank hesitated a moment. Then he stood up.

"You wait here," he ordered. "I'm going to sneak back in and get some paper. If I'm careful, Old Man Evans won't even hear me. He's lost to the world when he's composing."

Shad sat down on the edge of the boardwalk, letting his legs dangle down to the dusty road below. There was a hard lump of fear in his stomach, and his hands were damp. Somehow, some way, he had to learn this thing called an alphabet. If he didn't, he couldn't work at the *Sentinel* and earn sixty cents every week. It was a real job, and he knew he would never be offered another. All his hopes depended on this strange white boy, and everyone knew that most whites were changeable and subject to whims.

Frank returned almost immediately. He brought a stub of indelible pencil and a sheet of foolscap, which he spread on the walk.

"I never taught anybody the alphabet before, and I don't know how to start," he admitted. "I'll just have to write it down, and you can study it."

With Shad peering over his shoulder, he laboriously wrote the twenty-six letters of the alphabet.

"You'll need to learn the little letters, too," he explained. "But we'd better start with these."

"What do they say?" demanded Shad anxiously. "How do you tell them apart?"

"I'll start showing you now, and Mr. Foster will help you later," Frank answered him. "You can't learn the whole alphabet in one day. Nobody can."

"I can," insisted Shad stubbornly.

Frank smiled gently. "It's harder than you think. This is an A, and this is B, and this is C."

Shad repeated the letters, his eyes devouring the shapes. As they went along, he realized Frank was right. It was hard, but he was sure he could learn. He had to learn. Very few on the reservation could read. What a fine thing it would be to take back at the end of the year, the unraveled mystery of the white man's secret writing.

He had mastered the first five letters by the time Mr. Evans opened the door and shouted that he had finished his story about the untrustworthy apprentice. It was time to resume work.

Shortly before noon, Bertha appeared at the door, carrying a basket filled with Shad's lunch. She sniffed her disapproval of the cluttered print shop and departed without a word. Her appearance reminded Mr. Evans that he himself was hungry. He would go home to eat, he told them, and they would start the presses immediately on his return.

With a whoop of delight, Frank ran for his own lunch pail, but Shad sat on the floor, spreading out the foolscap beside him.

"What's the name of the next letter?" he asked. "It looks a lot like E."

"Eat, eat," urged Frank. "There's time for that later."

"No." Shad frowned, and his fingers traced and retraced the letters on the paper.

"I won't tell you anything else until I've finished eating," declared Frank. "It was a silly thing to try to do, anyway. I'm not a schoolmaster."

"Oh, no," said Shad quickly. "It was good. You are kind to help me. Not many would be so kind."

Frank was embarrassed, but he was pleased, too. As soon as they had finished eating, he was willing to continue the lesson. By the time Mr. Evans returned, Shad was working on G.

When the old Washington press was finally started up, Shad was too occupied to be bothered by the noise. Besides, as he told himself, it wasn't nearly as frightening as Tom Smith had led him to believe. It was clattery, of course, and awesome in the way it engulfed a plain sheet of white paper and covered it with black alphabet letters.

Shad carried stacks of the printed sheets to the long center table, where they would be folded for delivery. Each time he stared as he put them down, his eyes searching for the A's and B's and other letters he had memorized. He wondered when they would begin to say words to him.

It took Frank and Mr. Evans two hours to run off the two hundred copies required for the subscription list. Once, during the process, the press stopped entirely, and its owner, wrench in hand, dropped to his knees and disappeared briefly under the press bed. The failure was not serious, and he had it running again.

"Made good time." He sounded pleased as he announced the completion of the run. "I hope Ed Wheeler, wherever he lands, picks up a copy of the *Sentinel* and sees that we got along very well without him. You and Shad better fold papers before you wash the roller and put away type, Frank. Subscribers will start dropping in for their copies pretty soon. I'm going out for some air, but I'll be back."

Folding papers was easy, Shad decided, if you didn't mind a few paper cuts and getting your hands black. There were only four pages, which meant that each sheet was folded in the middle and once across. The stack before each boy grew taller by the minute.

"Hey, here's a story about you," cried Frank suddenly. "It's on the second page."

"About me? You mean my name's in the paper?" Shad could hardly believe it. He left his side of the table and came to stare down at Frank's pointing finger.

" 'Indian Boy Joins *Sentinel* Staff,' " Frank read aloud. " 'With this issue, Shadrack Youngbuck, a member of the Rogue River tribe, officially joins the staff of the *Valley Sentinel* as printer's devil. He replaces Frank Flint, who has been promoted to the position of apprentice, formerly held by Edward Wheeler, whose perfidious act of treachery has already been reported on page one. Ye Editor fully realizes that employing a member of the Indian race will cause comment and criticism from certain bigoted and prejudiced citizens of this valley. After due consideration, this scribe has decided that certain members of the Indian tribes from our nearby reservation should be given a chance to make what they can of themselves; ergo, the hiring of young Shadrack as printer's devil. He is the ward of Daniel Foster, Esquire, if any reader cares to lock horns with him!' "

"Does it really say all that?" asked Shad in an awed voice. His fingers traced the fresh ink, smearing it slightly. "Where does it say my name?"

"Here." Frank showed him. "And here's mine."

"What's going on?" Ralph Evans's voice sounded shrilly in their ears. He had come up behind them while Frank was reading. As they turned, they could see the lines of dismay on his face.

"I was just reading your story to Shad," explained Frank. "We'll finish folding the papers right away, Mr. Evans."

"You were reading it *to* him. That means he can't read it for himself. Dan'l never mentioned that when he talked to me." He shook his head despairingly. "It was a good idea. A fine idea. And I wrote a beautiful story. No one will dare criticize, not with that last line about Dan'l. But we can't have a printer's devil who doesn't know how to read. He can't put away type."

"I'm learning, Mr. Evans," Shad told him. "By next week I'll know the whole alphabet."

"He's down to G now," added Frank. "And I just started teaching him this morning. I'll put away the type until Shad's ready. I don't mind."

"You have learned almost a third of the alphabet in one day? And done your work, too?" Mr. Evans's eyes seemed to protrude even farther from his head. "Show me."

Proudly, carefully, Shad pointed out the letters he recognized on the paper. As he watched and listened, Ralph Evans's mouth gaped wider and wider with surprise.

"I can hardly believe it," he declared. "They always told me Indians couldn't take much book learning. There's many a white man in this valley who has to sign his name with an X, and you learned this much in one day."

"Then he can stay?" Frank voiced the question Shad was afraid to ask.

"Stay? Of course he'll stay. And the story of his learning the alphabet for the privilege of working on the *Sentinel* will be on page one next week!" declared Mr. Evans. "But the type is up to you until he's ready, Frank."

Frank nodded, grinning.

Shad looked at him gratefully. He had been wrong. Not all white boys were bad. Maybe the good and bad were equally divided, as in his own people.

Seven

"I'd be obliged if you'd come back after the parade and tote the picnic baskets to the park, Dan'l," said Mrs. Hicks. "I can hardly ask Jacob since he'll be eating with Doc and Martha."

"By rights you should take that meal off my board bill." Jacob Riley sopped up his egg yolk with the last biscuit. "I pay by the month, you know."

"If you feel that way, you can eat two picnic dinners—one with your brother, the other with us. Nobody's stopping you." She whisked the empty biscuit plate from the table and flounced to the kitchen.

"Maybe the Lord shouldn't have took that rib from Adam," said Jacob darkly. "Woman's been nothing but a thorn in the flesh since He created Eve."

"Might as well go downtown, Shad." Dan'l ignored Jacob as usual. "Parade won't start till nine o'clock, but we'll be there and ready when it does."

Shad followed him through the kitchen, fragrant with frying chicken, spice cake, and cherry pie, and into the backyard.

It was going to be hot again. The leaves drooped

on the maple tree, and the grass was parched and turning yellow. Still there was excitement in the air, which set the day apart. He was glad that the Fourth of July hadn't fallen on Wednesday or Thursday when he would be needed at the *Sentinel* office.

For Shad, the holiday had begun yesterday when wagons filled with people from the reservation, along with strings of mangy-looking horses, had arrived at the campgrounds. He and Dan'l went there after supper and had stayed so late that Mrs. Hicks complained about their night-owl habits.

While Dan'l visited with the older tribesmen, Shad spent the time with his friends, with Chicken and Dave Wachino, Mose Longman, and Ned Swan. Frank Flint was still his only friend among the boys in Evansdale, and it was a good feeling to be with young people again.

They wanted to know about his new life, but outside of his job at the *Valley Sentinel* and his ability to read the whole alphabet, he didn't know what to tell them. In just five months he had come to take the habits of the whites for granted. He traced A's and B's and C's in the dust, proudly saying the names, but the boys were more interested in what he had to eat and in his sprigged muslin shirt and leather shoes. Still, it was a fine evening, and the inner warmth remained with Shad even today.

"I've been asking around, trying to lay hands on a first reader," said Dan'l as they walked along. "Now that you know the alphabet backwards and forwards, it's time to get started on real reading."

"That would be fine." Shad's eyes glistened. He had discovered that there was more to reading than memorizing the alphabet. The letters had to be put together into words. He wanted to learn to do that. It was tantalizing to fold all those copies of the *Sentinel* each week and not know what the letters said.

"I been having a little trouble locating one, but Rufe thinks there's a reader around the house if Dulcy can lay her hands on it."

Shad's spirits sank. No matter how friendly her husband might be, Dulcy Gadsby still kept him at arm's length. Most of the women were that way. Mrs. Pugh and Mrs. Flint, Frank's mother, were friendly, and so was Martha Riley, but the others were reserved. He didn't believe Mrs. Gadsby would look very hard for the reader.

As they crossed Main Street, he could see the parade beginning to assemble at the school grounds in the block south of the Methodist and Baptist churches. There were flashes of bright bunting and white dresses as people milled around. Cody Pugh, carrying his coronet, hurried by, so preoccupied that he forgot to speak.

"Somebody should do something about our band," observed Dan'l thoughtfully. "They're eager and willing, but I swear they're all tone deaf."

When they neared Dan'l's office, they could see

that Rufe Gadsby had arrived before them. He had opened the door and brought a chair outside to sit in the sun.

"Morning, Dan'l. Morning, Shad. Fetch yourself some chairs and set," he called hospitably.

Shad hurried ahead, as a son should, and brought out two more chairs.

"You're out early, Rufe." Dan'l settled himself and reached for his pipe. "I should think the granddaddy of today's Miss Liberty would be needed at home."

"They sent me packing," Rufe admitted resentfully. "Such goings on at our house you never did see. Dulcy and Tine was up at daybreak, ironing her dress and combing her hair and getting ready. Now everything's done, and they got two hours to wait. Dulcy said for me to scat. She said I was making Tine fidgety."

"Doing what?"

"Just passing the time. I was telling her about past Independence Day parades, and how the Perkins girl fainted dead away from standing too long on the Liberty Wagon, and about the year Philena Peters near to fell off when she was Miss Liberty."

"What's the Liberty Wagon?" asked Shad curiously. Although he had attended these annual celebrations before, the Indians ignored the beginning of the parade. They were concerned only with the end, the horse races.

"Why it's only the biggest thing in the whole parade." Rufe was amazed that anyone would have to ask. "It's a wagon, Ed Cosper's finest, and pulled by four of his best horses. It's all fixed up pretty, and there's little girls in white dresses riding on it. Miss Liberty stands on top of the heap, and of course she's the most important of all. This year they picked my granddaughter, Clementine, and they couldn't have made a better choice. She looks right pert in her long white dress, made from a sheet, with her red hair all loose and hanging down. Tine's got nice hair. Gets it from me."

"Can't see what hair you've got left is red, Rufe," objected Dan'l.

"Well, it was once. Red as a love apple," said Rufe in a hurt tone. He patted the white circle of curls around the bare crown and glared at Dan'l.

"Dulcy manage to lay her hands on that first reader?" Dan'l changed the subject.

"No. I asked her, and she 'lows she don't know where she put it." Rufe was easily diverted. "Sure as God made little green apples, I seen that book not long ago, but I can't think where. Dulcy says she's not laid eyes on it for years, though."

Shad told himself that he had been right. Mrs. Gadsby didn't want to loan him the reader, and this was her way of evading the issue.

Main Street began filling with citizens who had come to watch the parade and with farmers and their families who had driven in for the day. They lined the hitching rails for three blocks or stood on the courthouse square. It was impossible for anyone sitting down to see over their heads, so Shad carried the chairs back inside, and the three squeezed in at the rail.

Promptly at nine, the parade began moving north from the school grounds. Shad found it interesting, although Dan'l had to explain parts of it. First came a decorated horse-drawn buggy driven by Pete Jackson, the mayor. It was followed by a second buggy containing Ralph and Mrs. Evans, representing his father, Ezekiel Evans, who had founded the town in 1847.

Next came two more buggies with Judge Clifford and Cyrus Boyd, the public prosecutor, and their wives. Sheriff Tombs chose to appear on horseback, but the animal's coat had been groomed to a sparkling sheen almost as dazzling as the polished star pinned to the rider's coat.

"Ralph going to read the Declaration of Independence again?" asked Rufe anxiously as the second buggy rolled by.

"No. Cyrus Boyd's reading it this year," said Dan'l.

"But Mr. Evans is reading a special ode that he composed himself," Shad volunteered. "Frank says he's been working on it for three weeks." He wondered why Dan'l, Rufe, and those who were standing close enough to overhear all groaned at his announcement.

Next came the band. It was composed of ten members of the community, who carried various types of musical instruments. They wore dark trousers and white shirts, with strips of red and blue cloth crossing their chests. They made a great deal of noise, but Shad was unable to recognize the melody.

The Liberty Wagon was last, and it was the best part of the parade. An open-bed farm wagon had been festooned with long strips of red, white, and blue cloth, and the team of four horses wore cockades of the same colors. Ed Cosper, resplendent in a blue coat and a high hat, which Dan'l said was to represent someone named Uncle Sam, handled the reins with a flourish, and the three sides of the wagon were lined with giggling, hand-waving little girls. They wore white dresses, and across each chest was a banner covered with alphabet letters. Shad couldn't read the words, but Dan'l said they spelled different states in the union, whatever that meant.

Clementine Gadsby, as Miss Liberty, stood on a platform in the center. Her long robe was of draped white cotton, and her red, unloosened hair fell to her waist. Occasionally she teetered a little as the wagon bounced in and out of a rut, but the smile never left her face. She held her torch aloft and nodded graciously in answer to the cheering crowd. Shad thought he had never seen anyone so beautiful as Tine Gadsby on the Liberty Wagon.

Since that officially concluded the parade, many of

the ladies began moving away, vainly trying to hold their small broods together. The men lingered on to watch the Indians.

There was a long wait. The Indians had not assembled at the school grounds, but were waiting in the park for a signal. It meant that now the parade would be reversing itself and coming from the opposite direction.

Shad was excited. His friends had told him there would be good horses this year. Betting had run high, and the favorite rider was a Molala named Ben Siliquois.

Ben was a quarter white. His grandfather had been a French Canadian, under John McLoughlin. He was a handsome man and had been much sought after by the girls on the reservation, but he had turned them all down. Instead, he had taken a wife from among the Rogue Rivers on the Siletz reservation near the coast. Her name was Maggy, and while she was neither pretty nor soft of tongue, she was the granddaughter of Chief Jo and owned four ponies in her own right. It was these ponies that Ben Siliquois would race this afternoon.

The spectators were growing restless at the delay.

"Won't be long now," Dan'l assured those nearby. "I say, they'll be coming any minute."

Even as he spoke, distant whoops of wild enjoyment rose above the gabble of the crowd. The riders turned the corner by the covered bridge, and the sound grew louder as they advanced down Main Street. Below the shouts and yells was the staccato of the speeding horses. Each hoof touched but briefly on the dirt road, spurting up a small circle of rising dust.

Shad's heart swelled with pride. These were his people, and in all the world he was sure there were no better riders. Each man was a part of his ungroomed mount, riding without a saddle, slung well forward on the horse's neck, and with only a guide rope for reins. The riders wore black wide-brimmed hats, which remained miraculously atop looped-up braids, and moccasined feet dug into the horses' bellies.

For a single stinging, dusty moment they were there. Then the shouts were floating back from the block beyond. They circled the courthouse square, then in a cloud of dust made their way back to the campgrounds.

"Land sakes, but them war whoops do bring back memories," admitted Rufe, mopping his head. "I can recollect the time when hearing them turned my blood to ice."

"It's all behind us now," Dan'l reminded him gently. "I say, it's all over and done with, and there's no call to hold a grudge. Come along, Shad. You and me have to tote Old Lady Hicks's picnic baskets."

The oratory was already under way by the time the two arrived at the campgrounds, for Dan'l had deliberately stalled with the baskets. On their arrival, he stopped well back of the gathering and lowered himself to the ground where a fallen tree could provide a back rest.

"We're late," he observed innocently. "I say, we best set back a ways where we won't bother the others."

After a moment, Shad sat down on the grass beside him, staring around curiously. Since the Indians always camped in the opposite end, next to Echo Creek, he had never seen this part of the grounds before.

In the center of a fine stand of oak and alder, the townspeople had made a clearing and erected a wooden building. It was open at the front and ends, with a back wall and roof. Steps led up to a stage from either side, and a tier of seats was occupied by those who were going to make speeches today.

Facing the platform, two sections of benches had been built. Weathered to splintery gray and built without backs, it was hard to imagine more uncomfortable seats, but here the citizens of Evansdale sat spellbound by the oratory.

Shad tried to listen, but the site chosen by Dan'l Foster was too far back to hear. He decided that Dan'l must have picked the spot deliberately, for the lawyer immediately dozed off into what proved to be a noisy sleep. Shad told himself that he might as well join his friends at the Indian camp beyond, but before he could do so, he, too, had fallen asleep.

He was awakened three hours later by Mrs. Hicks's resounding voice.

"I must say, you're a fine pair. Laying back there like a couple of toads against that tree!" She was standing above them, her perspiring face drawn into deep lines of disapproval.

Shad sat up guiltily, but Dan'l only opened one eye.

"Are they through, Mrs. Hicks? I say, is the oratory all done with?"

"It's over, and I must say Cyrus Boyd read the Declaration of Independence real good. Not that you couldn't have done better, Dan'l. You shouldn't always turn them down like you do."

"I get paid when I make a speech, Mrs. Hicks," he reminded her. "Is it about time to eat?"

"Past time, according to my innards."

She glanced around the clearing. The audience had left the benches, and crowds were hurrying in every direction as they searched for appropriate spots to unload picnic baskets.

"I think we'll stay right here," she announced. "We can unload the vittles on that tree trunk, Bertha, then fill our plates and set on the ground."

Bertha, who had been hovering in the background, silently stepped forward and lifted one of the heavy baskets. Mrs. Hicks seized the other, and after they had covered the fallen tree trunk with a cloth, they began to lay out food.

Although he had grown accustomed to Mrs. Hicks's hearty meals, Shad was unprepared for picnic fare. There was a crusty hill of fried chicken, brought in the bottom of an iron roaster since that was the only utensil large enough to contain the supply. There were jelly sandwiches and roast pork sandwiches and plain bread and butter. There was a vegetable dish of coleslaw and a pot of potato salad, aromatic with onions and decorated with rounds of hard-boiled eggs, and there were other boiled eggs with the yolks seasoned with fresh mustard, vinegar, and a dash of thyme from Mrs. Hicks's herb garden. There were cucumber pickles and crabapple pickles, with their stems still attached for convenient handles, and thin slices of pickled watermelon rind and end-of-the-garden pickles. There was a crock of baked beans, topped with slices of salt pork and glazed molasses. The three-layered spice cake was put together with brown-sugar icing, and the juicy triumph Mrs. Hicks called cherry pie oozed a delicate pink through the artistic tree she had pricked on the upper crust.

To wash it down, there was water that Shad carried up from the spring after Dan'l had showed him where it was. The citizens of Evansdale did not drink the water of Echo Creek, although the Indians found it good.

Long after they had reached the ends of their capacities, Mrs. Hicks kept urging more food on them.

"Look at all them good vittles. Before we get home,

they'll dry out and not be fit for nothing, especially the bread."

Shad, staring at the still loaded platters and dishes, remembered his friends and how curious they had been about the kind of food he ate. He would have liked to invite them here, but he knew that would never do.

"Mrs. Hicks, I have some friends at the campground. If the bread is just going to dry out anyway, could I take them a piece?"

"I don't know, Shad." She hesitated. "I wouldn't want to start a habit. I wouldn't want them to think that every time they come to town, they could expect free food."

"Pshaw, Mrs. Hicks," said Dan'l. "It's Independence Day. I say, it's a celebration. These are just young'uns, friends of Shad's. You wouldn't be starting a habit. You'd be handing out a little present in honor of our country's birthday."

"This time then," she agreed, after a moment. "But don't take just plain bread and butter. Take some with pork."

"Bet you a cooky them boys never tasted fried chicken," suggested Dan'l slyly. "Not the way you fry it, Mrs. Hicks. Few people have. I say, unless they've et at your table, they've never really had fried chicken."

"Go on with you, Dan'l Foster." She made a disparaging little sound in her throat, but Shad could tell she was pleased. "The drumsticks and good pieces of breast is all gone, but if they don't mind backs and wings—"

"They won't," said Shad quickly.

"Put in a few pickles, too," she urged. "And if you can carry it, there's still lots of cake left over that'll just dry up, too, setting in the sun."

When he finally joined his friends, Shad carried the iron roaster, heaped with food. They saw him coming, and guessing he had brought a gift, they ran to meet him.

"We better take this down the creek a ways." Chicken's black eyes glittered as he inspected the contents of the roaster. "We don't want anybody else to see."

"No. There's just enough for us," agreed Ned.

They found a spot on the curving bank where the brush grew so thickly that they had to force a pathway through. It was uncomfortable, for branches kept poking at them, and there were even a few blackberry vines to snag their clothes and hands. But they were out of sight and safe.

"Do you eat this way every day?" Mose's mouth was so filled with food that it was hard to understand his words.

"We have some of it every day." Shad smiled as he watched their enjoyment.

"You're lucky," said Dave. "Food like this to eat and fine clothes to wear. You make good friends, too?"

"Some," agreed Shad slowly. In his mind he began counting them off: Dan'l and Mrs. Hicks, Rufe and Doc Riley, Ralph Evans and Frank Flint, who was still his only friend among the boys. Sometimes, when he went downtown with Dan'l, a group of boys passed by, headed for the swimming hole, but Shad never looked at them any more. When he saw them coming, he always concentrated on what Dan'l or Rufe was saying and didn't look back until the boys were well down the block.

"I have more friends at home," he said at last.

"Besides, we smell better," Chicken reminded him, grinning. "I don't see how you stand it all the time, smelling the whites."

"You get used to it," said Shad. Chicken's remark came as a surprise. By now he was able to distinguish many of the things that went to make up the white man's odor. They varied with the sex and the individual: soft soap, camphor, liniment, mothballs, horehound, plug tobacco, cooking smells, perspiration, and the clinging, musty scent of unaired rooms. He wondered when he had stopped being conscious of them.

The boys spent the remainder of the afternoon together. They had a swim in Echo Creek, below the spot where they had eaten lunch. The brush kept any fussy white from knowing they had left their clothes on the bank. Then they walked back to the Indian camp to see how the betting was coming along.

Shad had heard the old men talk of bygone days before the Indians were herded onto reservations. There were stories of buffalo hunts beyond the mountains and stirring tales of war and raiding parties, where coups were counted. None of these things, he was sure, could exceed the excitement of a horse race, all that was left to the Indians.

Of the tribes settled on the Grande Ronde, only the Rogue Rivers originally had been horsemen. When they were brought here, forcibly by boat, their ponies had been taken away from them. The other tribes on the reservation were canoe Indians, but they owned a few nags. These the Rogue Rivers managed to secure, and little by little they acquired more. As soon as possible, they held a horse race, and when the other tribes saw how fortunes could be made or lost, they accepted the idea eagerly.

Everything they owned was bet on one race or another: produce from their farms, livestock, clothing, and food. Some would have liked to bet their women, but Dan'l Foster had convinced them that was bad. If any man bet a wife or daughter and the whites found out, the Indians would never be allowed to hold another horse race in Evansdale. They did not want that, of course. There were certain white men, generally those who hung about the Golden Bird Saloon, who bet whisky or money with the riders. Those were the best bets of all and should not be endangered.

There were ten entries in today's race, and eight were young men of the Rogue River tribe. Ben Siliquois, of the Molalas, and Aron Smith, of the Chinooks, completed the list.

"You still think Ben Siliquois will win?" asked Shad curiously.

"Ben's sure he will," said Chicken. "He's bet everything on himself. His land, too."

"Did Maggy let him do that?" Shad was surprised. Acreage itself was not usually wagered.

"Ben hasn't got a wife any more." Mose laughed. "Maggy divorced him."

"She threw his blanket out the door and went back to her father on the Siletz," explained Chicken. "She said she was tired of looking at a pretty face in an empty head."

"Ben was mad," added Ned. "He didn't care that Maggy left, but she rode one of her ponies. That left him with only three."

Late in the afternoon the Indians began leaving the park. Most of the whites had already gone, carrying their depleted picnic baskets with them. Those who cared to watch the races would do so from the square surrounding the courthouse.

By tacit agreement, the places beside the hitching rails were left free for the Indians on this occasion. Shad had just squeezed in between Ned and Chicken in a small spot before Dan'l's office when he heard his name being shouted from across the street. It was Mrs. Hicks, waving a black umbrella with which she had protected herself from the rays of the sun.

"Is that white squaw calling you?" asked Dave curiously. "What does she want?"

"I better go see." Shad was embarrassed, both for himself and Mrs. Hicks. It was unseemly that a woman should shout and make a spectacle of herself. And it was equally humiliating that an almost-man like himself should do her bidding. There was only one explanation that would satisfy his friends, and they would be sure to pass it on to the others later. He made it quickly. "She's the one who cooked the food you ate. Maybe she wants to give you more."

"Go," they all urged in a single voice, and Chicken added, "See if there is more of the sweet stuff you call cake."

Carrying Mrs. Hicks's empty roaster, Shad crossed the street. He was unhappily aware of the stares that followed him. Everyone from the reservation was there. Every eye watched his painful progress across the street in answer to the white squaw's bidding.

"I'm glad you remembered the roaster," said Mrs. Hicks approvingly when he reached her side. "Did your friends like the vittles?"

"Yes. They say thank you." He looked into her slightly sunburned face and remembered that she hadn't needed to send the food. She was smiling

113

kindly, happy that she had done something to please him. She had always been kind to him, he remembered, even from the first, defending him against the others to the best of her ability. Dan'l's support alone would not have been enough.

"Did you want me for something, Mrs. Hicks?" he asked.

"Yes," she said promptly. "I want you to explain the horse race to me. I watched one once and couldn't make heads or tails out of it."

"I'll try," he agreed politely.

Let the reservation laugh, he thought angrily. Mrs. Hicks would never know, and he didn't care.

Eight

❦

The horse races always began and ended before the doors of the Golden Bird Saloon. The course ran south for two blocks, turned east at the school grounds, then north before Mrs. Hicks's boarding house, rounded the perilous corner before Abe Flint's grist mill, thence back to Main Street and the finish. It was a short distance, but all the better for ponies that had more initial speed than endurance.

Shad tried to explain this matter of horse stamina to Mrs. Hicks as they walked back to the whites waiting in the square. The crowd was composed largely of men, but there were a few ladies in attendance. Tine Gadsby, still in her robes of Miss Liberty, had insisted on remaining to the end, and her grandmother, pink-cheeked with embarrassment, stood stubbornly at her side.

By this time the entries had turned the corner leading up from the campgrounds. Each man was astride a horse and led a string of extra mounts. They proceeded slowly up Main Street, and when they arrived before the Golden Bird, each dismounted and tied his horses to the rail.

"How come they got so many horses?" demanded Mrs. Hicks. "If they race that many, we'll be standing here a powerful long time."

"Not all those will race," Shad assured her. "Each man brings all his horses. He bets them all, and whoever wins will take them when it's over."

"Scandalous!" Mrs. Gadsby made little clicking noises of disapproval. "To bet is sinful."

"Shad, who is that tall one on the end?" Tine Gadsby leaned past her grandmother to speak to him. "We saw him at the campgrounds. He's very bold, the way he stares."

"That's Ben Siliquois." Shad wondered how Tine had encountered Ben. Some distance separated the campgrounds from the clearing where the whites had picnicked, and no Indian would go there.

"You've only yourself to blame, Missy," Dulcy reminded her tartly. "Nothing would do but you must show yourself in that Injun camp. I told you it wasn't decent."

"I wanted to see," insisted Tine. "I'm Miss Liberty, and liberty should go everywhere, even in the Indian camp. Besides, Grandpa and Mr. Foster were with me all the time."

Shad concluded that she must have paid her visit while he and the boys were swimming.

Across the street the ranks of Indian spectators parted, and a moment later the elegant figure of Floyd Chapman, proprietor of the Golden Bird, appeared at the rail. An elaborately tooled holster hung against one hip, the polished leather gleaming against the expensive black of his trousers. The ladies sniffed, but Shad thought he looked very grand.

"Ladies and gents!" Mr. Chapman had a bellowing voice that carried clearly across the street. "The racing is about to commence. Those that haven't made their bets had better do so now. You'll find a couple of the boys inside the Golden Bird ready to accommodate you. The first race will be a free-for-all once around the track."

The riders were stripped to the waist, and the muscles in their brown backs rippled in the glow of an orange sunset that gained luster from a distant forest fire. They were quiet as they led their selected ponies away from the rail and into the street.

"I wouldn't want you to take this personal, Shad," said Mrs. Hicks. "But I never did see such a parcel of mangy, scrawny nags in my whole life."

Shad smiled politely. He did not bother to tell her that often the owner of a horse rubbed mud on an animal's coat and burs in its mane and tail before a race. When people judged a pony's speed by appearance, as Mrs. Hicks had done, they would be apt to bet against it.

Floyd Chapman drew a formidable pistol from the holster and fired once in the air. Simultaneously each man was on his horse and the line had broken. There was a moment of pounding hoofs; then they were out of sight, concealed behind the square bulk of the Baptist Church.

Again Tine Gadsby leaned forward, and her gray, horrified eyes sought Shad.

"Did you see what that Ben Siliquois did just before he started out? He leaned down and bit his horse's ear!"

Shad shrugged. What better way to spur a horse to sudden speed!

Scarcely had the dust of their departure cleared away when they were back, screaming, beating at their ponies with sticks or knotted lengths of rawhide. Ben Siliquois was announced the winner of the first race.

The second race was exactly like the first, except that the distance was increased to twice around the track, and only horses that had never before entered a race were allowed to participate. Again Ben Siliquois won.

He did not qualify for the third event, a race for spotted ponies. Two of his horses were buckskin, and the third was a black. While it was going on, he sat on one of the buckskins, turned so he could watch the white spectators across the street.

"See," whispered Tine. "He's staring at me again."

"There's dozens of folks here. What makes you think he's picked you to stare at?" demanded Dulcy. "I'll be glad when this day is over and you braid up your hair and get into decent clothes."

Shad wished they would quit talking. He owed it to Mrs. Hicks to answer her questions, but white women who chattered of nothing should not be allowed at a horse race.

When the final scores were shouted, Ben Siliquois had placed first in all events except the spotted pony race. Shad knew the Indian encampment would be an exciting place for the next few hours, but he decided he had better stay away. His friends would ask why he had not brought more food, and the others would laugh because he had obeyed the orders of a squaw.

"That was real interesting," said Mrs. Hicks. "That Ben what's-his-name is a good rider."

"Too bad you didn't put a dollar on him, Dan'l," said Rufe slyly.

"If I had of, he'd have come in last," Dan'l told him. "I say, I learned a long while back not to bet on Indian horse races."

"Look!" gasped Tine. "There he comes now, Ben Siliquois. He must be looking for you, Mr. Foster."

Shad didn't think so. He had seen that look on the faces of young braves before, pride and resolve and another quality he couldn't quite name. Besides, why would Ben Siliquois come seeking Dan'l Foster? He wasn't in trouble. He had won most of the races and was now a rich man.

He came striding across the tall grass, straight to their little group, and his step was swaggering. The long braids, fastened around his head, had fallen down, and dust had collected on his face and bare back, clinging to the trails of perspiration and giving him a curious, tattooed appearance.

Dulcy clucked with disapproval. "Look at him, pushing white folks out of his way like he was their betters. Tine, you come straight along home." But she hesitated herself, and Shad knew that Mrs. Gadsby, too, was curious to hear what Ben Siliquois might have to say to Dan'l Foster.

"How, Dan'l Foster," said Ben. He stopped directly before them, and the orange sunlight glistened on his wet skin.

"How," replied Dan'l. He put out his hand, and Ben's dusty fingers closed over it. "You done some right smart riding, Ben. I say, you done real good."

"Ben good rider. Own many fine horses. Own much wheat, flour, many things. Ben rich."

"Reckon you are after today," agreed Dan'l pleasantly.

The Indian turned, and his eyes swept Tine Gadsby appraisingly.

"Girl belong to Dan'l Foster?"

Tine gasped audibly, and her grandparents stepped forward, forming a fat little wall of flesh before her. Shad understood now. He knew where he had seen that look he had been unable to identify before. It was the look of a young brave seeking a wife.

"No, Ben." Dan'l shook his head, the friendly smile still on his face. "She's not mine. I say, the girl belongs to Rufe Gadsby here."

Ben peered around Dulcy's bristling blue cotton shoulders.

"Girl *toke-tee yah-so*," he observed.

"Uh huh. The girl's got pretty hair, all right. Gets it from her granddaddy's side, he tells me."

"Hair!" shrieked Dulcy. "He's talking about your hair, Tine. I told you not to make a spectacle of yourself, letting it hang all day."

"You don't reckon he's figuring on scalping her?" demanded Mrs. Hicks in alarm.

"No," Shad assured her quickly. "He won't hurt her."

"Just what you figuring on, Ben?" asked Dan'l carefully. "I say, what you got in mind?"

Ben seemed to grow taller, and his lungs filled with a deep breath before he answered.

"Ben Siliquois mighty brave. Win many races. Own many horses. Very rich." Again he tried to peer around Dulcy Gadsby. "Ben give ten horses for girl."

Dulcy screamed, and Mrs. Hicks sputtered angrily, but before Dan'l could answer, Rufe had burst forward, waving a pudgy finger beneath the Indian's nose.

"Now, looky here, Ben what's-your-name!" he shouted. "You—"

Dan'l pulled him back, placing his own body between.

"She ain't for sale, Ben," he explained. "I say, her grandpa don't allow to sell her."

Ben nodded without changing expression and raised his offer. "Ben give twenty horses."

Twenty horses was a great price to pay for a squaw, Shad told himself in amazement. Brides did not usually come so high.

"Rufe Gadsby," screeched Dulcy. "If you're going to stand there and let that heathen offer you horses for your own flesh and blood—"

"Hush, Dulcy," warned Mrs. Hicks. "Leave it to Dan'l."

"No, Ben. Her grandpa don't want to sell her at all. I say, white men don't sell their women. Not for twenty horses, nor a hundred horses."

Ben did not understand. He appealed directly to Tine.

"Girl come with Ben Siliquois. Ben good to girl with pretty hair."

This time Dan'l's protests had no effect on Mrs. Gadsby. She rushed forward, beating on Ben's dirty chest with her small, plump hands.

Ben stood impervious to the rain of small blows, but Shad could tell that he was getting angry.

"Ben not go away," he said stubbornly. "Ben stay till girl goes, too. If white man leave Ben alone, Ben wait peaceful. If white man make trouble, Ben steal girl. If white man put Ben in jail, Ben get out. You remember. Ben speak truths."

He turned deliberately and retraced his steps across the street.

Most of the Indians had already piled back into

their wagons and started for the reservation. A handful, who had bet on Ben Siliquois, lingered on to conduct certain negotiations at the back door of the Golden Bird. These were the few who gave a bad name to the rest, and later most of them spent the night locked up in Evansdale's jail. Sheriff Tombs always turned them loose in the morning, sober, empty of pocket, and they meekly left for home.

Ben Siliquois was of neither group. After his talk with Dan'l, he collected his horses, now increased to thirty head, and led them south on Main Street. The town had not grown beyond the block containing the school. Rufus Gadsby's house was directly opposite, the last dwelling before the land reverted to a wild state. Here Main Street became the county road. Beyond several curves, it skirted the cemetery and led to farmlands and eventually the foothills of the Coast Range Mountains. Ben stopped at a grove of trees across from the Gadsbys' and immediately set up camp. He tethered his horses, erected a newly acquired tepee, and stowed away his supplies. He built a small fire, ate his supper, and then settled down quietly to wait.

Dulcy saw him out of her front windows and immediately sent Rufe to protest to Dan'l.

"Is he making any trouble?" asked Dan'l.

"He's scaring the womenfolks half out of their wits," Rufe told him. "And I don't mind saying, it gives me a turn just to see him there."

"He will do nothing," promised Shad. "Tomorrow

he will parade his horses, but he will not come near you. He will wait for you to come to him."

"There, now!" Dan'l smiled reassuringly. "You heard the boy. He knows all about it. I say, you got nothing to fear."

"I don't think Dulcy'll settle for that," said Rufe gloomily. "She's fit to be tied already."

Mrs. Gadsby was not only unwilling to settle—she was also most vehement in her demands that Ben Siliquois be removed from the grove of trees across the road. The other ladies of the community, fearing for the safety of their own daughters, joined her protests. Much to Shad's surprise, even Mrs. Hicks was of this mind.

"You go talk to him, Shad," she ordered. "See if you can make him see reason."

Shad knew it was useless, but he went to please Mrs. Hicks. As he had expected, Ben refused to argue the matter with anyone who had not yet reached manhood, but Shad got a good view of the camp.

"He's got lots of food and plenty of hay and oats for his horses," he reported to Dan'l. "He won't leave till it's all gone."

"Didn't reckon he would," agreed the lawyer. "There's nothing to do but sit it out."

Shad soon discovered that patience was not one of the white man's virtues. In fact, the behavior of the townspeople was something he could not comprehend. They acted as though Ben Siliquois was a whole tribe of warring braves instead of one man peacefully waiting some sign from the maiden of his choice.

Judge Clifford and Cyrus Boyd consulted certain law books and decided that Ben was trespassing. He must remove himself and his possessions from the grove or go to jail.

"Remember what he said," Dan'l reminded them. "He expects to go to jail, and when he's out, he might go so far as to steal Tine. I say, you best leave him be."

After much deliberation, Judge Clifford and Cyrus Boyd agreed that Ben Siliquois should be ignored. They tried to assure everyone that it was only a question of time until the Indian went away. They managed to convince some of the men, but the ladies were not appeased. No girl between the ages of ten and twenty was permitted to venture out alone. Doors were kept bolted, and the talk was of nothing else.

Shad couldn't understand that either. Ben didn't want one of the other girls, only Tine. He had made a generous offer, and unless he was pressed, it was unlikely that he would try to take her by force. Once brides had been stolen, but that was a long time ago. The custom had gone with the buffalo. Ben would just wait for Rufe to come to him. Then he would raise his bid. He tried to explain this to his new white friends, but outside of Dan'l no one believed him.

"Put him from your mind," advised Dan'l to the group of irate citizens. "Just go along like he wasn't there."

Such a thing was impossible, they insisted. Didn't the Indian lead his thirty horses up and down Main Street every morning and evening?

That was so they could drink in Echo Creek, Dan'l told them. There was no water in the grove, and both horses and Ben required water to drink.

Shad knew that the daily parades were partly to impress Rufe Gadsby with Ben's wealth, and he suspected that Dan'l knew this, too. Neither one of them said so. Feeling was running high enough as it was.

Tension had grown to the point where many of the townspeople included Shad in their resentment. It was because both he and Ben were Indians. Men who had always spoken to him on the street sometimes crossed over to avoid meeting him. At church, the ladies pulled their skirts aside to avoid brushing against him, and he could feel the curious stares of the boys even though he never looked at them any more.

At first he was hurt by this behavior. Then he burned with anger. He wished the year was over and that he was not pledged to stay.

Both Dan'l and Mrs. Hicks must have known how he felt because they were careful never to leave him alone, except on the days when he worked at the *Sentinel*. Frank Flint and Ralph Evans had not changed.

They were still the same. And Rufe, too, on his now infrequent visits did not seem to hold a grudge.

The Gadsbys had grown more frantic every day. Dulcy and Tine spent their waking hours peeping between the curtains of the parlor windows, which gave the best view of the grove. They would not leave the house, even to attend church services on Sunday, and they only permitted Rufe to leave long enough to make necessary purchases at Onnie Hatcher's store.

It was on one of these hurried shopping trips that Rufe again appealed to Dan'l for help.

"You got to do something, Dan'l." He put the basket containing Dulcy's groceries on the walk so he could wipe his face. "I feel like I'm in jail. Dulcy's at me from sunup till bedtime to get rid of that Injun. She wants me to shoot him if nothing else."

"You mustn't do that," cautioned Dan'l in alarm. "I say, that would be the worst thing you could do. Tell Dulcy I'll look in on her this afternoon. I'll think of a way. Leave it to me."

Rufe nodded miserably, picked up his basket, and trotted off. Shad looked after him unhappily. He wished people would believe him. Ben meant no harm. What he was doing was really a compliment to Tine's beauty.

"What are you going to do?" he asked Dan'l.

"I don't know. Thought maybe I'd ride over to the reservation and talk to Tom Smith. I say, him and some of the chiefs might be able to reason with Ben."

"He wouldn't listen," said Shad positively. "Ben's a rich man. Even before he was rich, he never listened to anybody but Maggy."

"Maggy?"

"He used to be married to her." Shad was surprised that Dan'l didn't remember. "She's granddaughter to Chief Jo from the Siletz. My friends say that she divorced him and went back to the tribe. It just happened a little while ago."

"Oh, *that* Maggy!" Dan'l's craggy face broke into a smile. "Know her well. Her pa and grandpa, too. You sure she married Ben?"

Shad nodded.

"She's some older than Ben, as I recall," continued Dan'l thoughtfully. "I say, she married late."

"She's fat and ugly," agreed Shad. "No one wanted her, even with her four ponies. Ben did not have to pay when he married her. I guess he was glad when she threw his blanket out the door and went home. They used to drive in to the store sometimes, and the way she talked to him made everybody laugh after they were gone. She called him lazy and good for nothing. Sometimes she even made him carry out the flour and put it in the wagon. Ben didn't like it, but he always did like she said."

"You should have told me before," said Dan'l reproachfully. "I say, we could have saved a lot of stew and fuss if I'd known about Maggy."

"But she divorced him. She's not married to him any more."

"That's Indian divorce. It won't stand up in court." Dan'l got to his feet. "We'll go tell Dulcy now and set her mind to rest. Then I'll hire a horse from Ed Cosper and start for the Siletz. Maggy'll take care of everything."

Through the folds of the front curtains, the Gadsbys saw them coming, and Rufe unbarred the front door, opening it a crack for Dan'l to slide through. When Shad innocently followed, Dulcy screamed. She rushed across the room and with flaying fists beat him back.

"He can't come in! He can't come in!" she shrieked. "I won't have a redskin in my house."

"But this is Shad," protested Rufe.

"If Shad can't come in, I don't neither!" Dan'l's voice cracked with anger. "What's the matter with you, Dulcy Gadsby? I say, we come to tell you we've got a plan to get rid of Ben Siliquois, and you act like we got the seven-year itch."

"He can't come in." Her face was very pink, and she looked close to tears. "He's just like that one across the road, only a mite younger. Who knows when he might turn on us? He's not welcome in my house. They're all alike."

"Grandma, they're trying to help us," cried Tine.

"Out!" ordered Dulcy, covering her face with her hands. "Out! Out!"

"We'll go," agreed Dan'l, with dignity. "But no firearms, Rufe. I say, if there's any more talk of firearms, I'll get a court order and lock the parcel of you up."

Across the road, Ben Siliquois had watched their brief excursion behind the Gadsbys' front door with interest. Before they returned to town, Dan'l stopped and spoke with him.

"You better give up, Ben," he advised. "The girl's not for you. I say, her grandpa won't sell her. Go back home. There's plenty of pretty girls on the reservation."

"Ben stay," the Indian insisted positively. "Next time give twenty-five ponies."

Dan'l was thoughtful as they walked back to the office, and Shad could tell by his narrowed eyes and the stubborn set to his jaw that he was still angry. He knew it was because Mrs. Gadsby had not wanted him in her house.

"You mustn't mind," he told the lawyer. "I don't care. She's never liked me. I shouldn't have tried to go in her house."

"You've never been inside her house before?"

Shad shook his head.

"Whose house have you been in? I say, outside of Mrs. Hicks, who asked you in?"

"Nobody." Shad tried to make his voice cheerful, but it was not the first time the thought had occurred to him. Even Mrs. Pugh and Mrs. Riley, who spoke cordially on the street, had never invited him to enter their homes.

The bristling brows dropped lower over Dan'l's eyes, but he made no further comment.

When they reached the office, Dan'l did not suggest bringing the chairs outside. Instead, he sat at his desk and motioned Shad to take a seat beside him.

"How'd you like to take a trip? I say, how'd you like to make a long journey through the mountains on horseback?"

"You mean go with you to the Siletz?" For a moment Shad was pleased; then his face fell. "I can't. Tomorrow I work for Mr. Evans."

"I'll take care of Ralph," promised Dan'l. "He'll let you off this week and be glad to do it. It'll give him a fine story for the *Sentinel*. 'Young Indian boy sets out on perilous journey to save womanhood of Evansdale in spite of the way they snubbed him before.' I say, it's right down Ralph's alley."

Shad didn't understand, but the prospects of a journey pleased him. It had been a long time since he had been on a horse, and despite its many fine points, Evansdale was a little confining.

"When do we leave?" he demanded eagerly.

"I'm not going," Dan'l told him. "I say, it's better that you fetch Maggy by yourself."

"But she wouldn't come for me," protested Shad. "She'll say she's through with Ben."

"Not when you tell her the divorce is no good,"

argued Dan'l. "I say, you tell her we'll go to court and I'll talk for her if Ben kicks up a fuss. You tell her he's a rich man now, with thirty horses and a barnful of wheat. And don't forget to tell her about Tine Gadsby and how he's up to twenty-five horses to buy her. Might even go all thirty. Three of them horses belong to Maggy. I say, she's not likely to overlook that."

No, Maggy wouldn't forget that. Shad could imagine her anger when she heard. Convincing her to return with him would not be hard.

"I hate to send you out alone," said Dan'l. "It's a long piece to the Siletz. Seventy-five miles or more, over the mountains."

That part was easy, Shad assured him quickly. There was a trail. It would be dry, and he could camp beside some mountain stream. The thought of possible loneliness did not occur to him. For centuries his people had gone on solitary missions. One who could not find enjoyment in himself and the land around him was to be pitied. The trip would take at least three days each way, possibly four, depending on the horse.

"We'll hire you Ed Cosper's best," promised Dan'l. "You better start out now."

Nine

❧◆❧

"The town of the whites is just ahead. We will be there long before the sun touches the mountaintops." Shad turned and shouted his announcement over his shoulder, then wondered why he had bothered.

Maggy had traveled this road before. She knew where they were as well as he. Perhaps he had lived too long with the whites, who were always filling a comfortable silence with obvious remarks that need not be said. It must be because he was returning to Evansdale that he was reverting to their ways.

Shad had spent a wonderful week and was a little sorry to have it end. It had been good to eat when he pleased and to sleep when he was tired, with the stars overhead and the night wind fanning his face. He was grateful for Mrs. Hicks's warm blanket when that wind grew chill, but equally thankful that he did not have to get up to face a morning of wood chopping, water carrying, weed pulling, and carpet beating. It had been pleasant not to have to smile when he did not feel like it, or to answer questions politely when he did not wish to speak. There had been times when the mountain trail had been steep and difficult to follow, but that was a challenge, and he was proud that he had found the way.

Mrs. Hicks had sent him off with more food than he could possibly eat, and a lot of it was still untouched by the time he reached the Siletz. He had preferred a supper of trout, fresh-caught from some mountain stream, and once he had feasted on porcupine, cunningly captured after the stupid animal had been tricked into shedding some of its quills. The porcupine had reminded him of Mrs. Hicks's roast pork, but there was a subtle difference that made it better.

Ed Cosper's horse had been a good beast, and Shad had spared it as much as possible by leading it up some of the worst slopes. All the Indians on the Siletz had admired it, and the fact that Shad had been trusted with so fine an animal had added to the respect with which he had been received on the reservation.

It had been a fine trip, and a successful one, for wasn't Maggy following along behind him on the trail? Dan'l Foster would be proud. And all the white people of Evansdale would be pleased, for now Ben Siliquois would have to leave. But Shad didn't care about that. He hadn't made the trip to fetch Maggy to please them. He had gone because Dan'l asked him to go. So far as the rest were concerned, it would serve them right if Ben camped in that grove forever. He wasn't hurting anything, anyway.

He smiled to himself, remembering his meeting and

talk with Chief Jo's granddaughter. At first Maggy had been angry when he told her Dan'l Foster said the divorce was no good and that she must return. Her black eyes had narrowed, and her many chins had firmed with determination. The ways of her father and grandfather were good, she declared. She would never go back to that lazy, boastful Ben Siliquois. Why she, a Rogue River, had ever lowered herself to marry a Molala, she could not imagine. For a time she must have become a woman without sense, but all that was over. She had returned to her own tribe, and Ben Siliquois could stay with his.

It was not until then that Shad mentioned the horse races. He had done it deliberately, saving that part for the last, although he knew it was not proper. The horse races should have been the beginning, and the whole discussion should have concluded with Dan'l's summons to return. But he had wanted to watch her face as she listened. Maggy had few admirers among her own or other tribes. Her sharp tongue made enemies, not friends. Shad had wanted her to refuse, then, after she heard the whole story, hear her swallow her own words in front of everyone.

Maggy had looked stunned when he told of her husband's success in the races. Her expression had changed to greed as Shad enumerated the many prizes he had won. It grew angry again when Shad reminded her that the three horses with which he had won those prizes belonged to her, and angrier still when she heard that Ben was trying to give everything away for a white girl with hair the color of rose hips.

"I will return with you," she declared loudly, ignoring the titters and laughter of the encircling Indians who had been listening. "I will take that Molala, my husband, back to the Grande Ronde. He is acting like a man without sense, and Dan'l Foster did well to send for me."

They left within two hours, Shad on Ed Cosper's horse, Maggy astride the black pony on which she had ridden to the Siletz.

He could not say she had spoiled the return trip for him. It was almost as though she weren't there. She was as skillful a rider as he, and tireless. She did not fill the air with senseless chatter, and at night she took over any necessary cooking. Nor did she treat him, as had Ben, like a boy, too young to be considered. They shared one aim, to get to Evansdale as quickly as possible. During their three and a half days together, Maggy had earned his respect. He even came to like her.

Now the journey was about to come to an end. It was all over. Ahead were people like the Hatchers and the Cliffords, who hated Indians and always would. And there were the women who believed it wasn't safe to invite him into their houses, and the boys who didn't think he was good enough to play with.

As he rounded the final curve before the county road became Main Street, a church bell began ringing. At first it tolled slowly, but suddenly it began to ring faster. A moment later it was joined by the second bell across the street. Shad wondered why. Late afternoon was an odd hour to ring church bells.

Behind him he was aware that Maggy's pony was shying at the unaccustomed noise, but he did not look over his shoulder. Maggy was a Rogue River. She could take care of a frightened animal as well as he.

He glanced to his right. Ben was still there, sitting cross-legged before the entrance of his tepee. Shad slowed his horse, motioning with his arm, but it was unnecessary. Maggy had seen him, too. She kicked her pony, urging it past Shad who waited in the road.

As she rode up, Ben got to his feet. The proud, resolute expression with which he had faced the citizens of Evansdale faded from his face. He looked bewildered and a little beaten. Shad couldn't help feeling sorry for him.

Neither her voluminous Mother Hubbard dress nor her many pounds of weight hampered the ease with which Maggy slid from her horse. At first she did not seem to notice Ben. She walked over to inspect the herd of thirty horses carefully. At some she nodded approval, but at others she shook her head scornfully. Shad knew she was thinking that no Rogue River would have accepted that horse in a bet.

Next she made a survey of the other acquisitions,

feeling the skins of the tepee, kicking at sacks of flour and oats with her moccasins. She examined two hats, a new coat, and unfolded the pile of blankets. Only then did she turn to speak to the man who had won all these trophies.

It was too far away for Shad to overhear, but he could see that Ben's lips did not move in reply. Instead, he stalked over to the horses and began adjusting lead strings. Maggy, meanwhile, was taking down the tepee, yanking loose pegs and slipping off the cover. She did not believe in losing time. The two would be on their way to the Grande Ronde within the hour.

Shad clucked to his horse in the manner of the white man, since it was what this animal understood, and rode on. For the first time he observed that the Gadsbys' front yard, within the neat picket fence, was crowded with people. He wondered what they were doing here. It must have something to do with the church bells, which continued to clang loudly.

He looked for, and found, Dan'l in the crowd and saw the proud smile on his craggy face. Shad smiled back. He was glad that he had fulfilled the mission his foster father had set for him. Later he would thank him for the pleasant trip, the chance to be away on his own for a few days.

Dan'l pushed forward, motioning for him to dismount.

"I knew you could do it!" Dan'l had to shout to make himself heard above the bells. "Evansdale is mighty proud of you, Shad, and I say, they should be."

"Did you have any trouble?" shrieked Ralph Evans, elbowing Dan'l out of the way at the fence. "Did the squaw come willingly?"

"Oh, yes," said Shad. He looped the reins around one of the pickets and moved toward the gate. "She wanted to come."

"But it was the way you told it," insisted Ralph. "It was your eloquent tongue that convinced her."

Shad smiled politely. He wasn't sure what the word eloquent meant.

"Why are they ringing the church bells?" he asked Frank Flint, who was holding the gate open for him.

"Why, for you," Frank told him, grinning. "People have been waiting all day. Yesterday, too, in case you got here early. The minute they saw you come around the curve, they were to start ringing the church bells. Slow, if you were alone. Fast, if there was somebody with you. That way everyone in town would know."

Shad stared at him in amazement. Was his errand so important that the townspeople would ring church bells?

A boy who could have been Frank's younger brother pushed forward.

"Ask him," he demanded. "Ask him now."

"I will," agreed Frank. But there was no time, for Ralph Evans elbowed him out of the way.

"How about wild animals?" persisted the editor. "I don't suppose you had a hand-to-hand fight with a bear?"

"No. I saw tracks and broken bushes where they'd been eating blackberries. I didn't see any bears. I heard cougars and bobcats at night, but—"

"You successfully eluded man's enemy by your greater wits." Ralph Evans nodded smugly. "Wild beasts were all about you, ready to pounce at any moment, but you escaped by virtue of your skill and cunning. I need all the facts I can get. I'm writing a long story about your trip for the *Sentinel*."

"We're much beholden, Shad," declared Rufe, grabbing his hand and pumping it up and down. "You've no idea what I been going through. And if it wasn't for you, it could still be going on."

"How was the trail?" asked Dan'l.

"All right."

"Steep," objected Ralph Evans, frowning. "And perilous. It climbed the tall mountains, dropping down into vast chasms where a man could be dashed below to his death."

"There were some high places with bad drop-offs," Shad agreed. "But I was careful."

"Exactly." Ralph beamed. "You had to be. Your life

was in your hands. And you, a mere boy, gambled that life for Evansdale's fair womanhood."

Shad's head was beginning to whirl. People swirled all around him, laughing, asking questions, pushing each other aside. They were acting as though he were a great warrior, returned from battle with many coups. And he hadn't done anything except ride to the Siletz and back.

"Now! Ask him quick!" It was the boy who looked like Frank, and this time he grabbed firmly onto Shad's arm so no one could come between them.

"This is my brother Will," explained Frank. "He wants to know if you'll go swimming with a bunch of us tonight in Echo Creek. Some of them wanted to ask you before, but you're always busy with Mr. Foster. I told them I thought you'd rather be with him so long as he let you. Grownups don't very often want to bother with us young'uns."

"Will you come?" demanded Will eagerly.

Shad grinned widely. He had time to nod before Will loosened his grip and stepped back.

A sudden silence had fallen on the group, and now a path was opened between Shad and the Gadsbys' gate. Coming toward him was Mrs. Whittelsey, wife of the Methodist minister, followed by her husband.

It was a great shock to everyone when Mrs. Whittelsey appeared in public, for she was known to be sickly and never went anywhere but to church.

"Shadrack," she said, walking straight to him and putting out her hand. "I congratulate you."

"Yes, ma'am." He took the pale, bony hand, then dropped it immediately. Mrs. Whittelsey's hands were unpleasantly moist. He had noticed that before, when she greeted the congregation on the steps after church.

"I would like to invite you to the parsonage," she said. "We will have tea and cookies in the parlor to celebrate this great thing you have just done."

"I'm afraid he can't come today, Mrs. Whittelsey." Dulcy Gadsby had finally found courage to leave her house. When she saw the minister and his wife on the path, she had hurried even faster. "For right now he's coming in my house to have milk and some chocolate cake Tine baked."

"Really, Mrs. Gadsby!" Mrs. Whittelsey sounded provoked.

"It's only fitting," insisted Dulcy stubbornly. "It was my granddaughter that he saved. Besides, he's been wanting a first reader, and just today I remembered where to lay my hands on ours."

Ten

᪥

"Whoa!" Shad pulled on the reins, and Nellie, Doc Riley's old horse, came to an obedient halt.

Shad looked over at Doc, who shared the buggy seat. His unshaven chin drooped on his chest, and even the jolting ruts of the road had not awakened him. For over a week the only sleep he had was when he answered country calls. Nellie was a good horse. She could bring him home safely, but she didn't know at which farmhouse to stop. Doc had hired Shad to do the driving so he could sleep both ways.

He looked so tired that Shad hated to wake him. He didn't have to, for the moment the buggy stopped rolling, a woman appeared on the porch and began shouting.

"Doc! Doc! Hurry! The baby's powerful bad."

Doc was instantly awake. He reached for the rusty black bag on the floor and resettled his hat.

"I'm here, Mrs. McBee. Don't take on now. I'm coming right in."

He followed the woman into the house, and Shad prepared himself for a long wait. Doc had admitted there was little he could do for the sick babies, but he always stayed a while to cheer the families. It was as much a part of a doctor's job to lift the spirits of the healthy as it was to heal the sick.

There was a strange malady going around Evansdale and the surrounding countryside that affected only babies. Shad wasn't too clear on the details, but the whites called it "summer complaint." Doc said they burned with fever, and the milk they drank went straight through them. They got no nourishment from it and soon became so weak that they could not fight the fever. Fourteen babies had died already, and there were more cases every day.

The August sun beat fiercely down, and the swarm of flies bit every time one lit on his skin. They were driving Nellie crazy, and her tail flicked constantly, trying to brush them off.

Shad turned the buggy and drove into the yard. He could see a watering trough beside a well. At least Nellie could have a drink. Maybe it would help her to forget the flies.

As he pulled up the bucket to fill the wooden trough, Mrs. McBee reappeared on the porch.

"Come in, Shadrack," she called. "Doc's going to drink some coffee before he goes. You can have some, too. You're welcome to sit right down in my kitchen with us."

Shad nodded. He had stopped being surprised at the many invitations he now received to enter the houses of the whites. Ralph Evans had done his job well. Even in the outlying farms, people had read the story in the *Sentinel.* He had gone home with Frank for dinner at the Flints, eaten cookies and milk inside Mrs. Riley's kitchen, been entertained by the Pughs, the Jacksons, the Boyds, and several other families. Mrs. Evans had invited him twice to meals, and he hoped she wouldn't again. People told the truth about her cooking.

There were a few houses, of course, where he would never be invited, among them the Cliffords' and the Hatchers'. Shad didn't care. No one could expect to be liked by everyone.

"I read all about you and them snooty town women," said Mrs. McBee when he reached the porch. "Don't you give them no mind. Light as thistledown, that's what they are, what with their sewing circles and their lodge doings. We're more solid out here in the country."

"Yes, ma'am," said Shad. He tried to imagine Mrs. Hicks as thistledown but couldn't. It didn't seem to apply to any other white woman he had met in Evansdale, either.

Doc was sitting at the kitchen table, drinking coffee from a heavy crockery cup. Mrs. McBee motioned Shad to a chair beside him and filled another cup from the granite pot on the stove.

"Main thing is to keep the baby warm," Doc was saying. "That's what we've got to do for a fever. Get her so warmed up that the fever will break out in a good sweat."

"I already got her wrapped in a heavy wool blanket, Doc."

"I see you have," he said approvingly. "You're doing just right, Mrs. McBee. With the good care you're giving her, she can't help but start to sweat any minute now."

Shad glanced at the cradle in the corner. Beneath the folds of blanket, he couldn't see the baby, but he could hear her gasping and moaning. He agreed with Doc. Any minute she would have to break out in perspiration. He was soaked through himself, and he didn't have a blanket, just the heat from the August day combined with the hot waves from the wood cookstove in the room.

The white man's treatment was not too different from the old Indian sweat bath, he concluded, only the baby wouldn't be dipped in a cool river afterward.

"Haven't you got no medicine for her, Doc?" asked Mrs. McBee anxiously.

"Best thing is sugar-water. For such a little tyke quinine's too strong, and she certainly don't need calomel." Doc's voice was soothing. "Don't give her too much. Maybe half a spoonful now and then."

"She'll like that." Mrs. McBee glanced at the cradle and smiled. "I'll give it to her right after she's nursed."

Despite his cheerfulness before the baby's mother, Doc sighed heavily as he climbed into the wagon.

"Don't you think she'll get better?" Shad asked in surprise.

"Not likely. She's got the look of all the others. But there's no sense in upsetting her ma beforehand. She'll find out soon enough, poor soul."

As soon as Doc had completed his country calls, they drove back to town. Shad let him out at his own door, where he could pick up messages that had been delivered to Mrs. Riley in his absence. Evansdale was small enough so the doctor could make his local rounds on foot, and he found it more convenient to stable Nellie in the town's livery barn, where someone else could take care of her daily needs.

Shad turned Nellie over to Ed Cosper, then cut across the courthouse yard to Mrs. Hicks's. It was midafternoon and he had missed dinner, but she would give him something to eat.

Mrs. Hicks was stringing beans on the back porch. She told him to bring his bread and meat outside and keep her company. To the accompaniment of popping beans, he had to tell her about Doc's country calls. Who was sick and from what, and what did Doc have to say about it when they left. She shook her head sadly when she heard of the McBee baby.

"Two more cases of summer complaint in town today, too," she reported. "And the Clifford baby's worse. Martha will tell Doc about it, and likely he'll be right over. I don't know what the judge will do if something happens to that baby. He sets such store by it. Almira Clifford waited fifteen years for it, and there won't be another."

Shad agreed it was too bad. He finished the bread and meat and considered going back for more.

"Why, there's Lucy!" declared Mrs. Hicks in surprise. "She's late this year. I been wondering about her. I need me a new clothes basket."

Turning in at the side path from the street was a familiar figure, and Shad's eyes brightened at the sight.

Lucy was a member of his own tribe, and a much respected one. Among the Rogue Rivers, women as well as men could become doctors, capable of driving out bad spirits, preparing medicines and poultices, and administering to the sick. Lucy was one of these. She was one of the older members of the tribe, so her chin was marked by three straight lines of blue tattooing, which ran from her lower lip to the turn of her chin. The custom was no longer followed by the young women, who had heard the whites designate those who wore the three straight lines as "One Eleven Squaws." While they did not know what it meant, the young Indians realized that tattooing was no longer admired.

Lucy was short and fat, so the wrinkles that would have been present in a thinner person had never formed. They were only about her eyes and in deep creases running down each side of her nose. She wore a calico Mother Hubbard dress that fell straight from her neck to her feet, and over her shoulder she carried a huge knobby bundle wrapped in a blanket.

"Greetings, Respected Woman," Shad called in the Rogue River tongue. He stood up politely, waiting for her to reach the porch.

Lucy lifted her head. The once black hair shone silver in the sunlight. She did not smile, but her dark eyes took on a new gleam.

"I'm glad you're here, Shad," said Mrs. Hicks. "You can do the talking. Lucy always makes out like she can't understand, but she's got no trouble saying how much she wants for her baskets. Tell her I want a big one to use for wet clothes, and I don't expect to pay too much for it, neither."

"It is you, Small Shadow," said Lucy when she reached the bottom step. "You have grown like watered corn in the sun, tall and straight."

"The Respected Woman speaks with soft words. She is kind."

"She is also tired," Lucy told him wearily. "I should never have come to this settlement of whites today. Everywhere I go, they turn me away with harsh words. They have no time to look at my fine baskets. They say there is sickness here."

"It is a sickness of babies only. Small babies. It does not strike older ones. It will not bother us."

"I am not afraid of the devils of sickness." Lucy frowned. "My power is still strong."

"What does she say about the clothes basket?" demanded Mrs. Hicks. "Has she got one in that blanket? I'd rather buy from Lucy than anybody. Her baskets last the longest."

"I'll ask," said Shad. He turned back to Lucy. "This is my friend, Mrs. Hicks. Her heart is good. She hopes you have a large basket for carrying wet clothes. She says your baskets are the finest on the reservation."

Lucy grunted. She put her bundle on the ground and untied the knotted corners of the blanket. It was filled with baskets made from willows and reeds, carefully laced with stout grass. They came in every size and shape, with handles and without, and some had darker grass laced in patterns among the light.

Mrs. Hicks put her pan of beans in the chair and came down the steps. As she approached, Lucy took a step backward, and her nostrils quivered slightly. Mrs. Hicks's hands explored the baskets, pushing them this way and that. At last her fingers closed on the largest of the lot, and she dragged it loose.

"This'll do," she announced. "Ask her how much."

"That is my finest basket. It took nearly a moon to make," Lucy told Shad. She looked at Mrs. Hicks and said clearly and in English, "Two dollar."

"Ridiculous," declared Mrs. Hicks firmly. "I never paid more than four bits for a basket in my life. Tell her, Shad."

"She said it took nearly a month to make, Mrs. Hicks," said Shad. It was a fine basket. He could see that for himself. "She says it's too much," he reported to Lucy sadly.

"I know what she said," Lucy told him coldly. She yanked the basket from Mrs. Hicks's surprised hands, replaced it in the blanket, and began doing up the corners.

"Very well," Mrs. Hicks said angrily. "I'll give one dollar, but not a penny more."

Once more Lucy began untying the corners.

"I'll go get the money out of the sugar bowl," said Mrs. Hicks. "You keep her here till I get back, Shad. Don't let her get away with my basket."

"It is a good basket and a fair price." Lucy's voice was pleased as she set the large basket aside. "I am glad that your friend, who smells so strongly of the whites, will have it. I may not sell another. No one else will talk of baskets on this day of sickness. I will go back to the camping place and wait until tomorrow."

"Do our babies ever get summer complaint, Respected Woman?" asked Shad. He told her of the McBee baby he had seen that morning and about Doc's saying that it would probably die.

"I have not seen the baby, so I cannot tell," she replied thoughtfully. "But I would not let it die. There are many herbs and barks. Each has its own use. I would choose the proper one, and the baby would live."

Mrs. Hicks came from the house, carrying a silver

fifty-cent piece and two quarters. She handed them to Lucy, who carefully bit each one to make sure of the metal. Then she handed over the clothes basket, raised her bundle to her shoulder, and without a word waddled off down the path.

"That's a pretty good squaw," declared Mrs. Hicks, watching her disappear around the corner of the house. "But I wish somebody'd tell her to take a bath."

Shad smiled to himself. He did not tell her that Lucy had found the smell of Mrs. Hicks offensive also.

When Doc Riley passed by after visiting the Cliffords, Mrs. Hicks called to him, asking about their sick baby.

"She may last the night, but she won't go through another." Doc sounded hopeless. His shoulders sagged with weariness. "I'm on my way now to Hen Peters. Martha tells me his baby was took sick this morning."

Mrs. Hicks clucked in sympathy. "I'll run over to the Cliffords' now and take them one of them fresh pies. Almira Clifford won't be cooking much, not with a sick baby. Maybe I'd better slice up some of that ham, too."

After she had gone, Shad sat for some minutes thinking of the babies. He wished that Lucy could see them. She had sounded confident when she said she wouldn't let them die. It seemed as though some unseen power had guided her steps to Evansdale today. He decided to follow Doc to the Peterses' and tell him about Lucy and her medicines.

He had to wait outside the gate a long while before Doc appeared. This time as he came down the walk, however, the smile remained on his face.

"How's the Peters baby?" Shad unlatched the gate and held it open.

"The baby's got a touch of it all right, but we started right off with sugar-water. This time maybe we've got a chance."

"There is a woman of my tribe in town." The words tumbled out as fast as Shad could say them. "She is a great doctor. She knows all the herbs and their proper uses. I told her of the sickness. She said she could cure it."

Doc smiled gently and patted Shad on the shoulder with one of his big hands.

"It's real nice of you to want to help, but I don't think folks would stand for no witch doctors around their babies. I'm doing all I can, and I studied medicine with Dr. Riggs, one of the finest, back in Illinois. If I can't cure the babies, well—maybe they wasn't meant to live."

"But, Doc—"

"I've got no time to argue, Shad." His voice was firm. "The Logans left word with Martha. I've got to go there next."

Shad stood staring after Doc's flapping coattails.

Perhaps he was right. Babies did die, even oftener than older children, but he couldn't forget Lucy's confident words. They stayed with him all the way back to Main Street.

"What's gnawing on you?" asked Dan'l curiously when he arrived at the lawyer's office. "I say, you look like a hound dog that just tangled with a skunk."

"It's the sick babies." Shad took the vacant chair on the sidewalk next to Dan'l. "Lucy said she could cure them, but Doc won't even listen."

"I seen Lucy across the street a while ago." Dan'l nodded thoughtfully. "She had a blanket load of baskets. What's this about her curing the babies?"

Shad poured out the whole story: what Lucy had told him about curing Indian babies and Doc's refusal of her help.

"Lucy didn't offer to help, did she?" asked Dan'l shrewdly. "I say, that could be just as big a snag as talking Doc into it. Lucy don't care much for whites."

"She likes you. She'd do it for you," insisted Shad. "And Doc says the Clifford baby can't last another night."

"Judge Clifford!" Dan'l leaned forward in his tilted chair, and the front legs came down on the walk with a thud that shook the boards. "You're not thinking of him, Shad! Hen Peters now or Pinkey Logan might be talked into letting their young'uns swallow some of Lucy's brew. Not Judge Clifford."

"His baby is the worst. It's going to die."

Dan'l hesitated a moment longer; then he got to his feet.

"Come along," he said. "We'll go find Doc."

At first Doc Riley was no more amenable to Dan'l's suggestion than he had been to Shad's.

"Folks would laugh me out of town," he declared. "Calling in an Injun witch doctor! Standing by while she capered around and yelled and shook rattles!"

"Lucy will not dance," insisted Shad. "She will mix herbs. The babies will drink, just like they drink your sugar-water."

"You know as well as anybody that some of them Indian remedies work, Doc," Dan'l reminded him. "Remember the time old Nat Grayson walked in out of the woods with a poultice of bird's-bill root on a gunshot wound? A squaw had fixed it for him, and he wouldn't let you touch it. When it finally did drop off by itself, there was hardly a scar."

"Nat was a grown man, not a tender babe," said Doc stiffly.

"And you've known a heap of others, too, old-timers who swore by Indian medicine. I say, it was all they had before you come."

"If the Peters baby takes a turn for the worse, he might take a chance," Doc agreed reluctantly. "Hen Peters' ma was a great one for home remedies. She never could abide calomel."

"It's Wade Clifford's baby that's up against it. And I say it's your duty to try to save that young'un, Doc, no matter what the means."

"Wade Clifford wouldn't stand for it. He wouldn't have that squaw in the house, and you know it. Do you expect me to go to him and say—"

"I expect you to do everything you can to save that baby," Dan'l told him severely. "I say, that's your duty. And if you stand by and let it die, knowing Lucy could have saved it, it will be on your conscience the rest of your life, Doc."

"How do you know she can save it?"

Shad could tell that Doc was weakening.

"I don't," said Dan'l honestly. "I say, nobody knows. But it's worth a try."

Doc nodded miserably. He agreed to meet them at the Cliffords' in an hour.

"Now, all we got to do is convince Lucy," muttered Dan'l as they turned away. In an even lower tone he added, "I hope you're right, Shad. I say, I hope your hunch is right."

Eleven

In the campgrounds, Lucy had set up overnight head-quarters. She had not brought a tepee, for she had hoped to sell her baskets and return home in one day. She sat on the ground, the knobby blanket, filled with baskets, at her side. Off a little way the horse she had ridden in from the reservation grazed quietly.

She seemed neither surprised nor especially pleased to see them when they arrived, but she was not unfriendly.

"How, Dan'l Foster," she said gravely, and although her eyes recognized Shad's presence, she did not address him. They had met earlier in the day.

"How, Lucy." Dan'l sat down on the ground oppo-site. From the pocket of his coat he brought out a small bag of hard candy, which he had purchased on the way.

Lucy accepted the gift and began eating the candy immediately.

Shad told himself that he must keep very still and let Dan'l do the talking. Lucy would not listen to a boy any more than Doc. She would not willingly help the whites, but if anyone could convince her, it was Dan'l.

"You have not sold many baskets today." Dan'l's bushy head bobbed in the direction of the knobby blanket.

Lucy grunted.

"You will sell none tomorrow, either." He spoke in her own tongue so she could not pretend to misunderstand. "There is a sickness here among the babies. They are dying from it. Their fathers and mothers will not look at your baskets until the babies are well."

Lucy sucked hard on the candy and frowned. Shad knew that she worked all year to make baskets. It was not right that the one day she came to offer them for sale no one was interested.

"Only after the babies are on the road to health will their parents look at your baskets," said Dan'l. "But the white doctor cannot cure them."

Lucy made a guttural noise in her throat. It showed her opinion of white doctors who did not bother to go regularly to the sacred mountain to renew their medicinal powers.

"The babies on the reservation are sometimes visited by sickness," suggested Dan'l. "Do they die?"

"No," denied Lucy firmly. "They do not die. I make them well."

"Could you make the white babies well?"

"Why should I?" she asked scornfully. "What are they to me?"

"The baby I am thinking of is very sick." Dan'l ignored her question. "It has been sick three days. The white doctor says it will die tomorrow. If you could cure that baby, it would show the whites what a wise doctor you are. They will buy all your baskets then. You need not cure all the babies, only one, to show them of your power."

"Three days is a long time." She hesitated. "It would be easier to cure one who had been sick a shorter time."

"If you can't do it—" Dan'l shrugged. He seemed to lose interest in the subject.

Shad waited, holding his breath. Perhaps it was too late for the Clifford baby. Perhaps Lucy should cure the Peters boy, who had only just fallen ill.

After a moment Lucy got to her feet. She hoisted the knobby blanket over her shoulders.

"I will look at this baby," she announced. "If it is too late to save it, I will know."

Dan'l consulted the large watch he kept in his vest pocket, secured by a heavy gold chain.

"By the time we get to the Cliffords' it'll be just about an hour," he told Shad in a pleased tone. "I say, we timed it just right."

Doc was waiting for them on the front porch, his ruddy face twisted with anxiety.

"I told you it wouldn't work, Dan'l. Wade Clifford won't let the squaw in, and Almira's in the back bedroom carrying on like she's lost her mind. Mrs. Hicks is with her."

"Have you told them there's no hope for the baby?"

"You know me better than that, Dan'l," said Doc reproachfully. "Miracles come rare, but one could happen. You best leave now, all of you."

Instead, Dan'l pushed past him and began pounding on the closed front door. Again Shad held his breath. He had seen Judge Clifford's temper before. The man could even appear carrying a loaded gun.

"Stop it, Dan'l," begged Doc. "I told you 'twas no good."

But Dan'l would not stop, and finally Judge Clifford opened the door a crack. His eyes were red-rimmed, and the long face above his black beard looked haggard, but to Shad's relief he was empty-handed.

"Stop that caterwauling," he demanded. "There's a sick child in here."

"A dying child you mean," corrected Dan'l. "Doc says your baby won't be alive this time tomorrow, Wade."

"Dan'l!" protested Doc as the judge slowly let the door fall wide. A moment later he stepped out on the porch.

"That the truth, Doc?" His voice implored Doc to tell him Dan'l was lying.

"It's true, Wade," said Doc sadly. "But it wasn't right of Dan'l to tell you like this."

"There's only one person who might save her, and that's Lucy here." Dan'l's head bobbed toward the woman standing at the bottom of the steps. "It may be too late for her to do anything, but we won't know till she has a look. What have you got to lose, Wade? Doc's done all he could."

After a moment the judge stepped back and motioned weakly toward the open door. He seemed to be stunned, Shad thought, like a man who has just received a heavy blow on the head.

Doc took the lead, and Dan'l motioned Lucy to come up the steps. Silently they entered the house, with Shad bringing up the rear. The judge remained where he was, leaning against the porch wall.

Mary Jane Clifford occupied a cradle in a small bedroom off the parlor. Like the McBee baby, she was closely wrapped in flannel.

Lucy set down her load of baskets and unwrapped the covering about the baby. Her brown hands were gentle as she lifted the tiny body carefully.

"Thin, like bones," she said. "She is dried out, this one, but it may not be too late. I will try."

"What did she say?" demanded Doc anxiously.

"She's going to try," Shad told him.

Lucy put the baby back in the cradle, but did not replace the blankets. When Doc moved forward to do so, she stopped him with a fierce frown and a few sharp words.

"The baby'll catch a chill," protested Doc. Then, as he saw Lucy's wide back disappearing through the door, he demanded, "Now where's she going?"

"To get bark," explained Shad. "She needs it to make medicine."

"I better go," declared Doc. "She's not going to pour something down the baby that I know is harmful. You come along, Shad, in case she talks. I can't make heads or tails out of it. Dan'l, cover up that baby while we're gone. I want her kept warm."

Lucy was walking calmly through the house and out the back door. As he passed through the kitchen at her heels, Shad could hear sobbing from behind a closed door, and the voice of Mrs. Hicks attempting to comfort Mrs. Clifford. It was just as well they didn't know what was going on, he decided. He doubted if either would approve of Lucy's medicine.

Outside, she stopped at the base of a tall fir tree that grew in the yard. In her hand she held a sharp knife, and now she began scraping away some of the heavy outer bark.

"What's she doing?" asked Doc in a puzzled tone.

Shad shook his head.

"The white doctor may watch," said Lucy scornfully over her shoulder. "It will avail him nothing. He will not hear the special words I say when I take the inner bark. You, too, must close your ears at that time, Small Shadow. It would be unwise for you to hear."

"I will do as you say," he promised fearfully.

When she had peeled off a square of tough gray bark, Lucy worked more carefully. The inner bark was white, tinged with green, and she peeled thin slivers, catching them in her palm. As she did so she spoke to the tree, explaining her need, but Shad put his hands over his ears. The mystic words and special phrasing were not for him to hear.

When her cupped hand would hold no more, Lucy turned and led the way back to the house.

"There's nothing poison about a fir tree," said Doc thoughtfully. "But a baby can't swallow them little pieces. It would choke to death."

Lucy halted in the kitchen, snapping out her commands.

"A container! Milk! More wood on the fire!"

"She wants a pan," explained Shad. "And milk. She's going to boil the bark."

Doc nodded. He seemed relieved that Mary Jane Clifford would not be given the splintery pieces. As he had said, fir was harmless, and milk was the approved food for babies.

Over the heat of the crackling fire, the milk soon boiled. The handful of floating bark gave off a sickly sweet odor that filled the room. It was a familiar smell to Shad. He wondered if he had once been given this medicine, but he could not remember.

After a certain time, Lucy removed the pan and carefully skimmed out the floating bits of bark. The milk was stained and discolored, and the aromatic smell stung Shad's nose as she handed him the pan.

"Give it to the baby when it is cool," she ordered.

"Let her drink what she can now. Later give her more. She must drink nothing but this until she is well. I have made plenty."

"We'll give it a try," promised Doc when he understood. "Leastwise, there's nothing here to hurt her."

Dan'l was still waiting for them in Mary Jane's room. Much to Doc's displeasure, he had not replaced the blankets.

"Figured she was warm enough," he told them reasonably.

"You ain't a doctor, Dan'l." Doc frowned as he hastened to tuck the flannel in securely. "I'll spend the rest of the night here. Looks like the Cliffords need me."

Mrs. Hicks, too, spent the night. Bertha served supper to Jacob, Dan'l, and Shad. It was a silent meal. No one could think of anything but the epidemic that was sweeping Evansdale, yet no one wanted to talk about it.

When he went to bed, Shad could see lights from the Cliffords' windows in the next block. He hoped that Lucy's medicine had been given in time.

Mrs. Hicks brought them the news they had hoped for at breakfast.

"Mary Jane is better!" She sat down in her usual place, and the look she cast around the table was triumphant. "No, no coffee, Bertha. I been drinking it all night."

"When did it happen?" asked Dan'l.

"Fever broke about midnight. That was the blankets Doc kept her wrapped in, of course, but the fir bark helped some because her stomach's easier. He told us what you done, Dan'l, and at first I was real put out with you. But so long as it worked out like it did, that's what matters."

"Blessed be the Lord in His great mercy," said Jacob Riley.

"Where's Doc now?" asked Shad. He was smiling, and he didn't feel that he would ever stop. "Does he want me to drive him this morning?"

"He 'lowed he'd stay in town this morning," Mrs. Hicks told him. "He's going to start everybody to peeling off fir bark and boiling it in milk. There's no denying that it's soothing to the stomach. This afternoon he'll make his country calls."

The smile faded from Shad's face. Without the proper words, he doubted if the bark of the fir tree would help too much.

"Soon as I've finished breakfast, I'm going to bed," said Mrs. Hicks. "You run along with Dan'l until Doc needs you, Shad. Bertha can handle things. We'll start no big jobs today."

As they came outside in the hot morning sunshine, Shad pointed across the street.

"Look! There comes Lucy. She's turning in at the Cliffords'."

"We'd better stop her," declared Dan'l. "They was up all night. It's no time for her to peddle baskets there."

Although they ran as fast as they could, they were too late. Lucy had mounted the steps and knocked on the door before they could arrive.

"Respected Woman, wait until later," called Shad. "Go some place else first."

"I'll buy a basket," offered Dan'l. "I say, a nice basket's what I always wanted."

Lucy did not turn. She stood calmly facing the door, and a moment later it was opened by Judge Clifford.

"Oh, it's you," he said in surprise. "Well, my baby's better this morning. It was nice of you to come and ask."

Lucy laid down her blanket on the porch and untied the corners.

"Lucy," shouted Dan'l. "The judge don't want to buy a basket now. I say, he was awake all night. I'll buy one, though."

"Of course I'll buy a basket," said Judge Clifford quickly. From his back pocket he drew out a black purse with a snap fastener. Shad watched as he shook out the contents into his hand. There was a small collection of silver and one coin worth five dollars. He pressed the whole amount into Lucy's extended palm.

"Take a basket," ordered Dan'l quickly. "She's no beggar."

The judge leaned over and picked up the smallest basket on top.

"Thank you," he said. "It's a fine basket. I will give it to my daughter. She will be proud to have it some-day."

Twelve

❦

Shad was surprised when Mrs. Hicks announced that he was to enroll in school that October.

"It's Dulcy's idea," she explained generously. "Since she gave you that first reader, she wants to make sure you make good use of it. And now that I think on it, I believe she's right."

He soon discovered that getting ready for school was no simple matter. First he had to have new clothes. His shirts had grown too tight, his pants ended well above his ankles, and again he was out of shoes. He bought new shoes from Onnie Hatcher, using some of the money he had earned at the *Sentinel*, but he didn't have to spend much for clothes. The ladies held another sewing bee. This was not confined to the Methodist group, for a great many Baptists wanted to contribute their services in making Shad's new wardrobe.

The day before the opening of school, Bertha heated water in the washtub and Shad was told to take a bath. After that, Mrs. Hicks gave him a haircut. She clapped a yellow bowl over his head and trimmed around the edges to make sure the line was straight.

He was a little fearful that first morning, but not about meeting the other students. By this time he knew most of the boys in Evansdale. Several times each week he went swimming with them in Echo Creek. Frank and Will Flint were still his favorites, but the others were friendly, too. They seemed to think he was some kind of hero, just for making that trip to Siletz by himself.

Sometimes Walter Hatcher was in the group, but he left Shad strictly alone. Walter didn't seem to have many friends. He was always criticizing someone and trying to stir up trouble, but only his eyes dared criticize Shad.

What worried Shad was the knowledge that he would be the oldest in the first grade. All the grades were in a single room, under one teacher, and everyone would hear his mistakes. He was afraid the others would laugh. To his relief, no one laughed. There were only five in his class, and since Shad already knew the alphabet, he was ahead of the others.

Mr. Short, the schoolmaster, was pleased and started him forming letters into simple words. He told Mrs. Hicks that Shad was as sharp as a tack and that it was too bad an Indian's brain stopped absorbing knowledge at the age of fourteen. If he had only started earlier, Shad might have been able to continue on through the eighth reader.

Mrs. Hicks said she had never entirely believed that story about brains stopping work. If it was so, Shad would just have to work twice as hard.

Shad studied as hard as he could, but it did not seem like work. He was eager to learn, and the weeks raced by. Almost before he knew it, they were into December.

Christmas came as a great surprise. Shad wasn't prepared for the presents he received. He wished he had known about Christmas presents. He had saved most of his wages, and it would have been nice to buy things for his friends, especially since they were so good to him.

Mrs. Hicks gave him a hand-knitted cap and mittens. Dulcy Gadsby brought over a knitted vest in stripes of red and black. Martha Riley embroidered his initials in the corners of half a dozen handkerchiefs. Ralph Evans presented him with a shiny new half dollar, and the Cliffords sent a fine leather snap purse with another fifty cents inside. But Dan'l's gift was the best of all. It was a Springfield rifle, the kind used by the soldiers.

"You ought to be able to bring down a deer with that," said Dan'l. "I say, it might even stop a bear if you learn to aim it right."

"I'll practice," Shad promised happily. "I'll learn to be the best shot on the reservation."

There was snow in December and early January, a thick white covering that bent the branches of the fir trees almost to the ground. Then one morning they awoke to hear rain drumming on the roof. A warm wind, called the Chinook, had blown in from the south. By nightfall the trees had dropped their white burdens, and the grass began to reveal itself in vivid green splotches.

"If this keeps up another day, Dave Tilford can put on an extra team and get his stage through from Salem," said Rufe Gadsby gleefully. "I declare, it's like living on a desert island when the snow's so thick."

"The mud will be as bad as the snow," Dan'l reminded him. "It will take ten horses to pull through all that mud."

Shad agreed. His people dreaded thick mud far more than snow.

"Six maybe." Rufe's round face puckered thoughtfully. "But I bet you a cooky Dave makes it through before the week's over."

On Saturday, the stage did get through, but it was three hours late. The horses were exhausted. It had taken six hours of hard pulling to cover fifteen miles.

A crowd of interested spectators awaited the arrival by the corner before the Golden Bird Saloon.

"See!" cried Rufe triumphantly. "I told you, Dan'l. It only took six horses."

"But look how late they are," Dan'l reminded him. "I say, if he'd put on ten, Dave might have made it on time."

"I hope he brought all the back copies of the up-state papers," said Ralph Evans anxiously. "It's hard not to have outside news to fill in with."

Shad stood on the sidewalk with the others. He couldn't understand their restlessness at being isolated. The people on the reservation took bad weather for granted. For weeks on end during the winter, each family was content to stay at home. If the farm roads in to the agency store were impassable, they ate what they had on hand. They didn't waste time worrying about what was happening elsewhere. They would find out in the spring.

Mud had splashed as high as the driver's seat, and when Dave Tilford climbed down, his face and clothes were so streaked that he was hardly recognizable.

"No passengers?" Ralph Evans's voice was disappointed as he attempted to peer through the chocolate-colored windows.

"No passengers," said Tilford. "But I'm paid to make the trip anyway, in case somebody wants to get out tomorrow. I brung the mail, though."

"I'll take it," called Onnie Hatcher. "As the duly appointed postmaster, you are supposed to turn it over to me."

"Only a couple of letters," reported the driver. "One for Judge Clifford. The other for Dan'l Foster. I got a pile of papers for you, though, Ralph."

"No need for you to carry my papers back to your

store, Onnie," insisted Ralph firmly. "You'll just make me wait while you read the headlines. I'll take them myself."

"And I will take my letter," declared Judge Clifford. "I want to get out of the rain."

"Might as well take mine, too," Dan'l said agreeably.

"It ain't legal," protested Mr. Hatcher uselessly. Ralph Evans already had his bundle of newspapers and was starting back to the *Sentinel* office. The stage driver personally delivered the two letters and began climbing back to his seat. He wanted to get his team to Cosper's Livery Stable as soon as possible.

Rufe and Shad followed Dan'l back inside. The fire crackled in the round iron stove, and the spittoons that Shad had cleaned last summer were rapidly filling up again. They hung their hats and coats on the wall, and Dan'l sat down at his desk to read his letter.

"Who's it from?" asked Rufe curiously. "Is it business or just the visiting kind?"

For several minutes Dan'l did not answer. He studied the white sheet of paper for a long time before he turned.

"It's from the warden over at Salem, Shad," he announced. "Your pa's year is up. I say, he'll be getting out on Monday."

Shad smiled, and a warm glow that did not come from the iron stove passed over him. His father was coming home! He would see him again. The year had gone by rapidly, but when he looked back, it seemed like a very long time. He wondered if his father had changed.

"You can't mean it!" Rufe's pink face puckered with distress. "You're not trying to say that Shad will be leaving?"

Dan'l nodded.

Shad looked from one to the other, and some of the warmth went away. He had not thought at first what it would mean. He would see Dan'l and Rufe and all the other good friends he had made only on rare occasions like the Fourth of July. He would never get through the first reader at school, much less the sixth. And he would never taste Mrs. Hicks's good cooking again.

"'Tain't right," protested Rufe. He stood up and walked over to take his wet coat from the wall. "Something's got to be done. I'm going home and speak to Dulcy about it straight away."

When his pudgy figure had disappeared, Dan'l opened the top of the stove and knocked the contents of his freshly glowing pipe into the fire.

"You and me'd better go home, too," he told Shad. "If Old Lady Hicks hears the news first from somebody else, she'll bust a pudding string. We best tell her ourselves."

Mrs. Hicks received the news that Lew Youngbuck was about to be released calmly.

"That's nice," she said. "I'm glad to hear that he's

paid for his sins. And I hope he learned his lesson so he won't be borrowing no more horses without asking first."

"Shad can remind him if he forgets," said Dan'l.

"Shad? How can Shad do anything about it?" She whirled around and glared at Dan'l indignantly. "Shad will be here in Evansdale. His pa will go back on the reservation."

"His pa will want Shad to go, too, Mrs. Hicks," he reminded her. "I say, he only loaned Shad to us for a year. The year's up."

"Fiddlesticks!" The pink spots of anger, which Shad had come to know so well, began to glow in her sallow cheeks. "Shad's going to school. He works for Ralph Evans Wednesdays and Thursdays afterwards. He belongs here."

"I'll come and see you, Mrs. Hicks," promised Shad. "Every time I come to town, I'll stop by."

"We'll see about that," she declared snappishly. "Don't nobody start crossing bridges before they come to them. Monday's two days off."

Next day when the stage left for Salem, it carried a passenger. Dan'l had announced his intention of meeting Lew Youngbuck when he was released Monday morning. The two would return to Evansdale on the stage that day, and Lew would spend the night in town. On Tuesday, Shad and his father could rent a couple of horses from Ed Cosper and ride west to the reservation.

As usual, Shad accompanied Mrs. Hicks to church. As he settled down beside her on the hard pew, he told himself it would be for the last time. If he ever returned, he would be an outsider. Perhaps no one would even speak to him then. It made him sad. He could hardly concentrate on what Mr. Whittelsey was saying.

"Don't take off your good clothes," ordered Mrs. Hicks as they walked home afterward. "Leave them on. We're going to have company right after dinner."

"Who?" asked Shad curiously.

She shook her head, closing her lips tightly. He would have to wait to find out.

Dulcy and Rufe Gadsby were the first arrivals. They came even before Bertha had finished clearing the table, and Mrs. Hicks ushered them straight into the parlor. Shad could tell that it was to be an important gathering, for the parlor was seldom used.

Next came Mr. and Mrs. Cyrus Boyd, closely followed by Ralph and Mrs. Evans. Sheriff Tombs and his wife arrived with the Cliffords, and Bertha and Shad had to scurry to bring in the dining room chairs so that people could sit down. Still they kept coming, the Rileys, the Flints, the Whittelseys, Reverend and Mrs. Blake from the Baptist Church, the Peterses, the Cospers, the Albrights, and the Pughs.

The Hatchers did not come, and one or two other families who sided with them, but the people Shad knew best and liked the most were all there. The chairs ran out after a while, so the men stood and the ladies sat. From time to time all eyes kept straying to Shad. He had never felt so bewildered in his life.

"It's getting late." Judge Clifford cleared his throat and rapped for order on the back of his wife's chair. "I propose that we get started."

"Hear, hear!" cried some of the men, while Mrs. Clifford beamed with pride that her husband was to be in charge.

"It has come to our attention that one of our community is about to take his leave of us," said the judge, looking significantly at Shad. "In the year that he has spent in Evansdale, he has contributed a great deal to the welfare of this town. In the beginning, I have to admit there were some of us who resented his being here. I was one of them. But that has changed. He has wormed his way into our hearts and our affections, and we do not wish to see him go."

At first Shad could not believe that the judge was speaking of him. Then, as he saw the nodding heads and the smiling faces all focused on his own, he knew. They had come to pay him honor and to say good-bye. His throat filled with emotion, and he willed himself to keep back unexpected tears.

"Moreover, we do not intend to let him go," continued the judge loudly. "Shad, we want you to stay here with us."

"There'll be no board money," said Mrs. Hicks. "You more than pay your way with the work you do for me."

"And if she gets tired of you or you of her, you're welcome to move to our house," called Dulcy Gadsby.

"In two years I promise to get you through the fourth reader, maybe into the fifth," said Mr. Short.

"And there's your job at the *Sentinel*. We'll make it full time whenever you want," promised Ralph Evans.

"The thing is nobody wants you to leave, Shad," added Martha Riley in her gentle voice. "We love you. We want you to stay here with us for as long as you want to."

Shad stared at the circle of white faces. They wanted him to stay, to be one of them. They were his friends. Then their features began to mist over, to blur before his vision, and he turned and ran from the room. He couldn't let them see him cry, not even if they were tears of happiness.

Thirteen

"Could I leave school at noon today, sir?" asked Shad.

"It is not Wednesday or Thursday when you work at the paper." Mr. Short frowned over the top of his spectacles. "Why should I excuse you early on Monday?"

"I want to meet the stage. Dan'l will be bringing my father."

"Will he indeed?"

Mr. Short had attended yesterday's meeting in Mrs. Hicks's parlor. He knew all about Lew Youngbuck's expected arrival, Shad thought resentfully. Why should he pretend to have forgotten?

"There will be time to visit with your father at the close of school," said the schoolmaster firmly. "I see no reason why you should leave your studies early. You will find, Shadrack, that great changes will have taken place in the past year. Your father has been locked up in prison. You have had the advantages of living with the whites, of being accepted by them. I fear the two of you will have little in common now. Whatever you have to say to one another will not take long."

179

Shad stared at him in amazement. Before this he had always respected Mr. Short. The schoolmaster was smart. He knew everything there was to know about reading and writing and numbers. Apparently he knew little about people. Shad would have a great deal to say to his father. He would have to explain about the whites asking him to stay with them. However great the opportunity, Lew Youngbuck would have to give permission first.

He felt the anger well up within him. He wanted to strike out at this stupid white man, but he forced himself to speak calmly.

"Then I'll go now," he said. "I won't wait till noon."

Mr. Short gasped and reached out to clutch at his coat, but Shad pulled away. As he left, he could hear titters from the students. They had enjoyed hearing him talk back to the schoolmaster as he had.

The rain had stopped when he stepped outside, and the clouds were blowing away, showing a soft blue sky beneath. The wind was still cold, and he pulled his collar close about his neck.

Across the street Mrs. Gadsby was sweeping her front porch. She saw him and beckoned vigorously. Shad crossed over to see what she wanted.

"Are you sick?" she called anxiously as soon as he was in earshot. "Why are you leaving school?"

"I'm not going today. My father's coming on the stage, and I want to be there to meet him."

"You'll want to tell him about your good fortune right away," she agreed, smiling. "So much has happened to you that sitting in school today would be a waste. I'm surprised that Mr. Short had the sense to see it, though. I didn't figure him to be that bright."

"Yes, ma'am," said Shad politely.

"Come in," she suggested. "I baked fresh cookies. You got all morning to kill before the stage is due."

Shad followed her inside, down a short hall, past the closed door of the parlor, and into the combination sitting and dining room beyond.

"Set by the fire," said Dulcy hospitably. "I'll fetch the cookies."

While he waited, Shad looked at the pictures on the wall. There were a great many, some of flowers, others of scenery or animals. Under the glass of the largest frame was an artistic wreath of many-shaded artificial flowers. Tine had told him once that the flowers were made of bits of human hair, snipped from the heads of friends and relatives, many of them long dead. It was a nice memento, she said, and Shad agreed. Human hair was a nice reminder of the dead. That was why the old Indians took scalps.

"You're admiring my hair wreath, I see," said Dulcy when she returned.

"Yes, ma'am," agreed Shad. "It's beautiful. I'd like my father to see it. He likes pretty things."

Dulcy almost dropped the plate of cookies.

"Now, Shad," she said reproachfully. "You know I

can't have your pa in here. He's not the same as you. He may not be at all like that Ben Siliquois that stirred up all that trouble last summer, but I dasn't take a chance. After all, he did do time for stealing."

Shad looked away. Even if his father had meant to keep the horse, not borrow it as Dan'l said, he had taken it from a stranger. Lew Youngbuck would never steal from a friend.

"Now you mustn't take it to heart," said Dulcy firmly. "It wasn't meant for you. You're different. You're a good boy, and everybody likes you. Here, have a cooky."

Shad ate only one. It was tender and rich, but he found it hard to swallow. He left as soon as he could.

Since Dan'l was in Salem, he did not even stop at the office. Instead, he made his way to the *Valley Sentinel*. Ralph Evans and Frank were always glad to see him.

The editor was at his desk, composing a story for the next issue, and could not be disturbed. Frank motioned Shad to the farthest corner where they could talk in whispers.

"What's Mr. Evans writing about?" asked Shad.

"About you. And how you're going to stay here and be like a white man. You should read it. The old man's really laying it on. It's about how smart you are and how the *Sentinel* saw it first and gave you your chance."

"I'm not smarter than anybody else," protested Shad, but he was pleased just the same.

"Old Man Evans says you are. He says you're smart enough to turn your back on the reservation now that you've got a chance to get out. And that's being smart, isn't it?"

Shad stared at him hard. Was that what they thought he was doing, turning his back on his own people? Most of the whites in Evansdale had become his friends, but he had other friends, too.

He made an excuse to leave as soon as he could.

As he walked slowly back on Main Street, he studied the town thoughtfully. He knew it well by now: the courthouse set in the center of the block, with the Hanging Tree beside it; the row of buildings on his right, Onnie Hatcher's store, the barbershop, where Mr. Albright paused in his work to wave a soapy razor in greeting as he passed by, Dave Peacock's carpenter shop next to Dan'l's office, and the Golden Bird Saloon on the corner. He knew them all, and they had lost their wonder and surprise for him. They had become a part of his daily life, and it could be so forever if he willed it.

Mrs. Hicks was taking freshly baked pies from the oven when he arrived home, and she looked at him sharply.

"Why ain't you in school? You sick?"

"No, ma'am. I asked Mr. Short to let me out early. I

want to meet the stage." It wasn't a real lie. He had asked Mr. Short's permission, even though it had been denied.

"Anxious to tell your pa the news, are you?" She nodded wisely. "Well, I made up an extra apple pie. You can take it with you when you go to meet the stage. It's for your pa to eat tonight."

"An apple pie for my father?" Shad smiled. He never should have doubted Mrs. Hicks.

"Figured he might savor it. Dan'l'll likely pick him up something else at Onnie Hatcher's, but one of my apple pies should go down real good while he's waiting for morning at the jail."

"At the jail?"

"Dan'l always arranges for the Injuns to spend the night there when it's late," she reminded him. "He'll do the same for your pa. You don't need to worry."

"No," said Shad slowly. "I guess not."

Since there was always the chance that the stage might be on time, Mrs. Hicks let Shad eat dinner early. It was wasted effort, she declared, inspecting his half-touched plate.

"You're just too wrought up to eat. Might as well run along and wait for that stage. And don't forget the pie."

The clearing sky had brought many of Evansdale's citizens outside to witness the arrival of the stage, but the biting wind was driving a few back in.

Shad took the apple pie to Dan'l's office and set it

down on a pile of papers on the desk. He was joined almost immediately by Rufe Gadsby.

"It's nippy, even in here," complained Rufe, rubbing his hands. "Why don't you build up a fire? It'd be a comforting thing to welcome Dan'l back."

Shad agreed and prepared to do so at once. With a knife he began slicing curls from several sticks of kindling so they could catch more easily.

"Guess you're some anxious to see your pa," said Rufe, sitting down and pulling the coat collar close about his neck. "You got exciting news to tell him."

"Yes," said Shad. He crumpled a sheet from an old copy of the *Sentinel* into the cold stove and dropped the kindling on top.

"There's something you got to keep in mind, though." Rufe spoke slowly, choosing his words. "Remember your pa's a changed man. Not the way you remember him at all."

"What do you mean?" asked Shad in amazement.

"Well, you've got to expect that a year in prison's bound to leave its mark on a man," explained Rufe. "He never gets over it, Shad. Folks will always think of it when they look at him, and he knows it. They won't never forget. It'll follow him all his life, and sometimes after he's dead, too. Sometimes his young 'uns have to bear the shame."

"You mean that when people look at me, everyone will think of my father?" asked Shad. "They'll remember that he was in the penitentiary for a year?"

"No, not you," objected Rufe quickly. "You're different, Shad. Folks knew about your pa long before they got to liking you. I was just speaking about people in general."

Shad waited for the flames to catch on the kindling before he began putting in wood. On the reservation it would be very different. People didn't care if you had been in prison. When you returned, life began again where it had left off.

"Nothing like a good fire on a cold day," observed Rufe. "Wonder if the stage will be on time today. I can't digest my dinner proper till I see what comes in on it, and that means Dulcy has to hold back her meal. She's getting sick to death of the stage being late, let me tell you."

The stage arrived at one o'clock, and Dan'l was the first one off. He nodded and smiled in response to the greetings of the crowd, but his blue eyes searched for Shad, standing by the office door. When they found him, he smiled even wider, then turned back to the stage. Lew Youngbuck was already climbing out.

Shad caught his breath with relief. Rufe had been wrong. His father hadn't changed. Oh, he wore a new suit. It was ill fitting and of shabby material, but the cloth in the coat and trousers matched, and it hadn't cost anything. It was provided by the state. No braids swung below the black hat. They had been cut off, but that didn't matter, either. They would grow again. And the brown skin was paler than usual, which was natural in a man who had not known sun and rain and wind for twelve months. But the proud lift of the shoulders was what counted, and the way he carried his head. His unsmiling scrutiny of the white faces gathered on the boardwalk was as it had always been. They could never change his father!

Dan'l made his way through the crowd, pausing to shake an occasional outthrust hand, and Lew Youngbuck followed. They came straight to the doorway where Shad was waiting.

"Hurry in, Dan'l. There's a nice fire going," called Rufe, who was leaning against the door jamb. "We got a heap to tell you, me and Shad. Wait till you hear! And Dulcy, she stirred it up in the beginning. It was all her idea."

"You can tell me outside, Rufe." Dan'l opened the door and gently pushed Shad and his father inside. "I say, this is private now, between Shad and Lew."

"You come, too, Dan'l," pleaded Shad. "I need you."

The lawyer did not ask questions. He entered the office and closed the door firmly in Rufe Gadsby's outraged face.

"You have grown tall," said Lew, inspecting his son approvingly. "Soon we can no longer call you Small Shadow. We must give you a new name."

"We've been calling him Shad." Dan'l crossed to the desk for his tobacco can. "I say, some folks make it Shadrack, but Shad's good enough for me."

"It was your right to give him a name in this year that he was your son," said Lew courteously. In answer to Dan'l's motioned invitation, he accepted one of the chairs around the stove. Then he turned again to Shad. "Dan'l Foster tells me you have been a good son and have earned the friendship of some of the whites."

Shad could stand it no longer. He could not wait. The problem that weighed so heavily on his mind had to come out.

"They asked me to stay here. Nearly everyone in town came to Mrs. Hicks's yesterday after church, and Judge Clifford made a speech. They want me to go to school, and Mr. Evans says there's a full-time job at the *Sentinel* any time I want. Mrs. Hicks says there'll be no board money, either."

Lew Youngbuck received the news quietly. The smile was gone from his face. He seemed to be considering the matter. Finally Dan'l broke the long silence.

"But you don't want to stay," he said.

"I can't stay," Shad told him. He hadn't been sure before, but suddenly he knew. "They're trying to make me into a white, but I'm not a white. I'm an Indian. I belong with my own people."

The dark eyes beneath his father's hat glowed with pride, but still he said nothing.

"Then it's all settled," declared Dan'l mildly. "I say,

so long as you've made up your mind, that's all there is to it."

"But I haven't told them," confessed Shad miserably. "I didn't say anything. They just took it for granted that I'd want to stay. And at first I thought I did. Now I know I can't."

Dan'l nodded, tamping the tobacco well into his pipe.

"I'll never make them understand," continued Shad. "They'll hate me. Unless you talk for me, Dan'l, the way you always do. You can make them see that I am grateful for all the things they've done for me—that I love them all and still want to be their friend."

"I'll talk for you," promised Dan'l. He smiled at Shad reassuringly. "I say, they've all forgotten you was just a loan for the year. Some of them's likely to take it mighty hard, though. Old Lady Hicks, for instance. She's mighty fond of you, Shad. Don't you think you ought to talk to her yourself?"

Shad swallowed a lump that had formed in his throat.

"It is better that I do not see my white friends until the passage of another moon has dulled their feelings." Unconsciously he had lapsed into his tribal tongue. His eyes pleaded with Dan'l for understanding. "If I told them now that I could not stay, they would first try to persuade me with soft words. When that failed, their hearts would fill with anger, and there would be more words which would always stand between us."

"I reckon you're right," agreed Dan'l. "When folks get riled up, they're apt to say things they don't really mean. And they can never call them back."

"They keep saying that I am different. That is so of everyone. You are different from Rufe Gadsby and Judge Clifford and Jacob Riley. But in one way you are the same. You are white. I am Indian. I cannot turn my back on my own people. I am one of them. But I will try to be good, one who brings honor to the tribes. Perhaps some of the things I learned this year among the whites will help me to do that."

"You were already good of heart," Dan'l told him. "You didn't need the whites to improve on that. But maybe the year has made you understand us a little better. It's too much to hope that it will work the other way around."

"I'm sorry not to say good-bye to Mrs. Hicks." Shad spoke slowly, reverting to English. "Tell her I love her most of all. And tell her that my father and I thank her for the apple pie. We will eat it tonight together."